VEGAS WEDDING, WEAVER BRIDE

BY
ALLISON LEIGH

MILLS
BOON

First Published in Great Britain 2017
By Mills & Boon, an imprint of HarperCollins*Publishers*
1 London Bridge Street, London, SE1 9GF

© 2017 Allison Lee Johnson

ISBN: 978-0-263-92320-9

23-0817

Our policy is to use papers that are natural, renewable and recyclable products and made from wood grown in sustainable forests. The logging and manufacturing processes conform to the legal environmental regulations of the country of origin.

Printed and bound in Spain
by CPI, Barcelona

A frequent name on bestseller lists, **Allison Leigh**'s high point as a writer is hearing from readers that they laughed, cried or lost sleep while reading her books. She credits her family with great patience for the time she's parked at her computer, and for blessing her with the kind of love she wants her readers to share with the characters living in the pages of her books. Contact her at www.allisonleigh.com.

For my husband.
Always surprising and ever holding my heart.

Chapter One

Las Vegas, Nevada

Penny Garner stared at the piece of paper Quinn Templeton was holding between his long fingers. Her stomach, which had already been hovering somewhere two floors below her feet, sank even farther.

She clutched the white bedsheet closer against her naked body, trying desperately to pretend that Quinn wasn't just as naked. He simply wasn't bothering with a sheet to hide anything. From the top of his rumpled, dark-haired head to the long, vaguely bony toes on his feet, he was entirely, utterly, gloriously bare.

And he didn't seem the least bit shy about it, either.

Which left Penny two choices.

Focus on him, or focus on the piece of paper he'd found on the nightstand next to the bed.

And the piece of paper—disturbing as it was—seemed safer at the moment. "*What* is that?"

Quinn flicked the official-looking document onto the bed that stood between them. The tumbled bed that Penny had scrambled out of only minutes earlier, dragging the sheet along with her. "You can read."

She *could* read. But that didn't mean the marriage certificate, lying with lopsided innocence against one of the bed pillows, made any sense.

She unwound one arm from the sheet to reach out for the sheet of paper. "It's not real."

She picked it up. Studied her signature on the line that said "Bride." *Penelope Garner* was looped across it in familiar, lopsided cursive. The "Groom" line was similarly obscured under Quinn's slashing signature.

She looked up at him. Then just as quickly away. When she'd been fifteen, she'd had a crazy mad crush on him. So much so, that she'd thrown herself at him. Tried, in her juvenile way, to seduce him. He'd been home on leave from the air force. She'd been living with her latest foster family, the Bennetts, across the street from where his parents lived.

At the time, he'd ruthlessly crushed her immature advances.

Now she wished she still possessed some of the outrageous guts she'd had in her youth. Because it was more than a little mortifying to be knocking on the door of thirty and feeling wholly out of her depth when faced for the first time with a seriously naked, gorgeous man.

A man with whom she'd spent the night.

A man with whom she'd signed a marriage certificate.

She sank onto the edge of the bed. Which at least gave her the advantage of turning her back toward him.

"This has to be a joke. Right?" It was hard enough to believe she'd *slept* with him. But marry? She set the certificate on the mattress beside her and wound her shaking hands inside the sheet twisted around her. "It looks like my signature. But I don't remember signing it. Do you?"

"No."

If she concentrated on the paper hard enough, then maybe she could forget the way she'd wakened.

Wrapped in his arms.

Intimately.

Fortunately, she'd come to her senses and scrambled out of bed, dragging the sheet with her.

Unfortunately, that was about the time he'd noticed the marriage certificate. And his brows had pulled together in the fiercest frown she'd ever seen.

Her fingers worried the edges of the sheet clutched above her breasts. "Then it's got to be a joke."

The fancy Las Vegas hotel suite had thick, plush carpet that easily swallowed the sound of Quinn's footsteps as he rounded the bed to her side. "Who would play a joke like that?"

She averted her eyes before she got too much of an eyeful of his muscular nude body. He'd been injured during his latest deployment. Had spent months in the hospital, she knew. It didn't seem logical that he could be so tanned all over the way he was. The only pale skin he possessed was—

She made herself look away again.

"I don't know!" All her frustrated confusion sounded in her voice as she raked back her hair. "Your cousins? Your sister?"

"Maybe Viv?" His deep voice turned mocking. "God knows little old ladies like my recently discovered granny are prone to pulling off pranks like this."

She made a face at him, only to get distracted yet again by all that…nakedness. She could only imagine how his *granny* would react if Viv knew her personal assistant had gotten into mischief with her grandson on what was supposed to be Vivian's get-to-know-each-other-better trip with her grandchildren. "Would you *please* put on some clothes?"

"I remember a time when you wanted me to take 'em off." But mercifully, he moved out of her sight again.

"Yeah, well, I was a kid," she muttered. A wild, willful kid who'd only been trying to find her place in a world that seemed to have no place for her at all. "And if you were any sort of gentleman, you wouldn't remind me of that."

He snorted softly and sat on the side of the bed right next to her. "I'm not a gentleman."

She peeked at the blue jeans now hugging his thighs and breathed a little easier. At least as easily as she could, considering his bare shoulder was brushing warmly against hers. "You're in the air force. Isn't being a gentleman a requirement?"

He didn't answer that, but plucked the crumpling piece of paper from between them and held it between his hands. "At least you're not jail bait anymore," he muttered. "What's the last thing you remember from last night?"

She felt her cheeks getting hot.

They were sitting on the edge of a hotel room bed. It was painfully obvious *what* had happened last night. Her imaginative mind had no trouble whatsoever filling in the blanks.

And wasn't it ironic as all get-out that she'd finally shed her virginal state, but couldn't actually remember a single detail of it?

Even as a teenager, he'd inspired insanity in her. As an adult, clearly nothing had changed.

Flushing even hotter, she pushed off the bed, dragging

the unwieldy sheet with her. "I remember the nightclub." His grandmother had been adamant that Penny join them. "I remember your grandmother kept ordering bottles of champagne." Penny had been a little concerned. In addition to being the woman's personal assistant, she was supposed to be watching out for Vivian's health.

But Vivian had also been surrounded by five of her fully adult grandchildren. If they'd been cheering on their fully capable grandmother, how on earth could Penny have intervened?

"Viv does seem to like her champagne." He pushed off the bed, too, grimacing a little as he straightened. He pressed his hand to his side, covering the long surgical scar there as he paced around the bed again, coming to a stop in front of the enormous sliding glass door that opened to a narrow balcony with a spectacular view of the city below. His hand went from his side to the window as he looked out.

The August sun was shining brightly outside the glass, and the sunlight threw his body into perfect relief. From the spread of his wide shoulders to the narrowness of his hips where the blue jeans clung a little too precariously, the only flaws he possessed were that long zipper-like scar and a scattering of small pale blotches on his side.

"Last thing I remember was dancing with you." His thumb tapped the window. "We'd been at the bar. Champagne's not usually my thing. I ordered a pitcher of margaritas for the table." He seemed to be talking more to himself than her.

She felt perspiration spring out on her forehead. "It can't be a real marriage certificate."

"Yeah, well, unless we prove it one way or another—" He broke off when there was a knock on the door.

His eyes were as dark a brown as his hair and they

looked toward her, questioningly. Combined with the whiskers blurring his jaw and the faint lines arrowing out from his eyes, it was a powerful combination.

"How should I know?" she whispered. "This is *your* suite."

She'd been the one to make all the hotel arrangements for Vivian's little Las Vegas jaunt. Quinn, his sister, Delia, his triplet cousins and Vivian were all on the same floor. Penny's room was twenty floors below. Down in the less outrageously expensive section. Vivian had thought that particular touch was uproariously funny.

But then Vivian Archer Templeton had more money than Midas. She could afford expensive vacations like this for half her family anytime she wanted.

The knocking got louder, this time accompanied by feminine laughter. "Come on, Master Sergeant Templeton," came the muffled voice through the door. "Get your lazy bones moving. You're going to be late for lunch."

Lunch.

Penny groaned. Vivian was expecting everyone in her suite for the lunch that Penny had arranged the day before. It was to be their last full day in Las Vegas before heading back home to Wyoming.

"They're gonna get a kick out of this." Quinn started for the door, but Penny grabbed his arm, feeling sheer panic flow through her veins.

"You can't tell them!"

He lifted a dark eyebrow. "How do you know they don't already know?" He held up the certificate. "Maybe they were our wedding guests."

She felt the blood drain out of her face. He was right. If neither one of them could remember the events of the previous night, how could she assume anything? "Don't bring it up if they don't," she whispered fiercely. "Promise me!"

His eyes searched hers.

The knocking on the door got louder.

"Your leave is going to end. You'll go back to your life," she reminded him. "I'll still be in Weaver. I don't want the notoriety, okay? Gossip is the town's best industry."

His beautifully molded lips compressed. He looked like he wanted to argue.

"Please, Quinn. I'm begging here."

"Fine." He sounded none too pleased about it.

Relief still flooded through her. One thing she knew about Quinn Templeton was that he always kept his word.

She dashed around the bed, snatching up the items of her clothing that were visible, and raced toward the bathroom, only to nearly fall on her face as the sheet caught around her feet.

Quinn's hand shot out, grabbing her arm and righting her.

"Quinn!" The knocking on the door hadn't ceased.

"Dammit, Greer, I heard you the first time," he said loudly. "Keep your pants on!" He pushed the crumpled marriage certificate into Penny's hand and nudged her gently toward the bathroom. "Be more careful," he murmured.

She ducked her chin, grabbed the sheet higher around her calves so she wouldn't trip again and hurried into the luxuriously appointed bathroom, closing the door quietly after her.

The sight of her reflection in the wall-size mirror made her shudder. Guilt. Horror. Shock. All of that was in her face. Added to her rat's nest hair and the whole bedsheet thing, she looked exactly as she'd expect a woman to look after waking up in a strange man's bed.

Only he wasn't really a stranger, was he, if she'd known him since she'd been a teenager? Or was that negated by the fact that—aside from his brief visits home to Wyoming—he'd been gone for more than the last decade?

She dumped the certificate, her dress and the one high-heeled sandal she'd found beside the bed on the marble counter and pressed her ear against the closed door.

All she could hear were muffled voices.

She raked her tangled hair away from her face. It was only then that she noticed the narrow band on her left finger. It was gold. Set with sparkling diamonds that circled all the way around. And it was beautiful.

She slid it off so fast it flew out of her fingers and rolled out of sight.

Her conscience nipped at her and she crawled around until she found it. Feeling decidedly nauseated, she set it on top of Quinn's leather shaving kit, then went to sit on the side of the enormous round bathtub. Pins prickled behind her eyes and she pinched them closed. It was one thing to know she'd slept with him. But how could she have *married* him?

Once upon a time, she was supposed to have been a bride. A real one. Only instead of marrying Andy, she'd—

"Hey—"

She looked up to see Quinn had opened the door. He'd added a T-shirt over his jeans. The light gray cotton looked stretched almost to breaking point over his shoulders.

"You all right?"

She swiped her cheeks. "You ever hear of that thing called privacy?"

"That's what locks are for." His dark, dark eyes roved over her. "There's no reason to cry. At least my cousin Greer didn't mention anything unusual. This isn't the end of the world."

"Waking up married?" She waved her hand, only to feel her sheet slipping, and yanked it once again up to her neck. "Sure. Nothing to be worried about at all."

He scrubbed his hand down his bristly jaw. The thick, wavy hair on his head was as dark as ever, but the whiskers there definitely held a touch of gray.

She wished she could say they detracted from his appeal.

But at least that long-fingered hand of his wasn't sporting a wedding ring.

"We'll figure it out," he said.

"I don't know how you can sound so calm." She hitched up the long ends of the sheet and stood. "This is a disaster." She slipped past him to return to the bedroom area. As oversize and opulent as the bathroom was, it was still too small with him in it.

His voice turned flat. "Stop being melodramatic."

She spotted her other shoe peeking out from beneath the gold silk bedspread that was hanging off the mattress, and grabbed it. She couldn't remember how the evening had ended the night before, but she distinctly remembered how it had started off—with her fully clothed and wearing her usual complement of panties and bra underneath.

"Maybe it's not a disaster in comparison to your usual life." She knew he was part of some special operations thing in the air force. To Penny, that was just code for some really dangerous thing in the air force. "But it is to mine. I have no desire to be anyone's wife. Certainly not like this." Not to another man already married to the military. She'd been through that before. Thanks to the army in which Andy had served and a close encounter with an IED on his way home for their wedding, she'd never even had the opportunity to be a widow. *Much less a wife.*

She went down onto her hands and knees to look under the bed. But the ivory carpet there was smoothly vacuumed and untarnished by discarded undies. She sat back on her knees.

"What are you looking for?"

"The rest of my clothes, obviously." She hitched up the sheet again and stood. "I need to get back to my room. Clean up. Make sure everything's set for the flight home tomorrow."

"What about my grandmother's lunch?"

"That's for all of you. I'm the hired help, remember?" She shoved her long hair away from her face again as she walked back into the bathroom, carrying her second shoe.

She shut the door.

Pushed the door lock for good measure.

She dropped the sheet and pulled her stretchy dress over her head, dragging the dark purple fabric down over her bare hips and thighs. She hoped it wasn't too obvious that she was entirely commando under the dress.

She raked her fingers through her hair, trying to restore a little order to the dishwater-blond mess, and splashed water over her face, using one of the plush towels stacked on a glass shelf before she pushed her bare feet into her high-heeled sandals and opened the door again.

Quinn was leaning against the wall opposite the door, his arms folded over his wide chest. "Feel better?"

She could feel herself flushing, but she gave a brisk nod anyway as she walked out of the bathroom. Without high heels, she was taller than average. With them, she stood close to six feet, putting her generally eye-to-eye with most men.

But not Quinn. He was still several inches taller than she was.

Which was a completely irrelevant point, she reminded herself as she scanned the room, hoping to spot her purse, because she truly did not want to have to go down to the lobby and get a new room key. Not looking the way she did.

Her relief when she finally found it half-hidden among the ivory leather couch cushions was almost comical. Her room key was tucked safely inside one of the pockets, exactly where she'd put it before joining Vivian and her family for dinner the evening before.

She felt her eyes drifting toward the bed and yanked them front and center.

Quinn hadn't left his position against the wall. Which meant she had to walk past him once again to get to the door of the suite.

"You can't run far, Penny."

"I'm not running. *You*, however, are supposed to be sitting down to lunch with your grandmother." She opened the door.

But he reached out and closed his hand around her wrist before she could leave. "Viv can wait. It's not every day I wake up to a wife."

Heat rushed up her throat into her face. "I'm not your wife."

His eyebrows lifted. "Really? I know they say what happens in Vegas stays in Vegas, but we're talking marriage here. And we've got a certificate that strongly suggests you're most definitely my wife."

She didn't know if it was deliberate or not, but his thumb was pressed right against the racing pulse in her wrist. "Then we'll get another certificate that undoes it!

Annulments must be almost as popular in this state as weddings."

"Annulment means there's been no marriage—or anything associated with the marriage—at all."

"That's right." She pulled on her wrist, but his fingers held fast. They weren't hurting. But they weren't giving so much as a centimeter.

Instead, he reeled her in closer. He tucked one finger beneath her chin, and her mouth went dry.

He turned her face until she was looking back into the hotel suite.

Right at the bed.

"You sure an annulment is going to be all that easy?" His voice was low. Intimate. "We have a consummated marriage here, sweetheart."

A flush ran through her veins, and her skin seemed to tingle.

"We don't know that for sure," she reminded, wishing that she sounded a lot less hoarse and a lot more certain.

His callused thumb moved slowly over her inner wrist. "You don't remember the way we woke up?"

She wanted to block out his words as badly as she wanted to block out the truth. Because she did remember exactly the way she'd awakened.

Engulfed in his warmth. His hand on her breast. His hair-roughened thigh between hers.

He hadn't been inside her. But he could have been. Everywhere she'd been soft and wanting, he'd been hard and insistent.

And for a moment, a wonderful, blissful moment, she'd imagined Andy weren't dead. That he was there with her. They were together, finally, just the way they'd planned to be.

And then she'd realized the dream wasn't a dream at all. But a nightmarish reality.

Because it wasn't Andy's arms surrounding her, causing her to feel so deliciously safe and cherished. It wasn't Andy's soft blue gaze and sweet smile she saw when she opened her eyes.

It was Quinn.

Quinn, with the seductive grin, and the devil-dark eyes that had always made her want to do anything and everything with him. Sanity had thankfully kicked in then, and she'd jumped out of bed like the hounds of Hades were nipping at her feet.

"I don't care what that marriage certificate says. And I don't care what went on in that—" she swallowed hard "—that bed. I am not your wife. You are not my husband. We are *not* married."

Then she finally twisted her wrist free and rushed through the doorway to escape.

Chapter Two

Quinn sighed, watching Penny race away from him. Her golden-streaked brown hair bounced around her shoulders. Her shapely hips swayed with every step.

Then she reached the end of the hallway and turned with almost military precision and marched out of sight altogether.

She didn't look back at him.

Not that he'd expected she would.

He rubbed his hand over the throbbing pain inside his head and turned back into the hotel suite.

The digs his grandmother was footing the bill for were a helluva lot more luxurious than what he'd been used to for pretty much the last two decades. He couldn't say that he didn't appreciate all the comforts.

He did.

Nor could he say that he'd been overly disappointed waking up to find a beautiful, sexy woman draping her long legs and long hair all over him.

Because he hadn't been.

Not until clarity had come blinking into Penny Garner's startlingly blue eyes, and she'd bolted out of his arms as if he were the worst sort of snake alive.

If he'd *really* been a snake, he'd have taken what she'd offered all those years ago when she'd been just a precocious, well-developed teenager.

He wasn't a snake. But he also wasn't going to apologize for the way they'd woken up in this fancy hotel suite, tangled together. Because—he was thankful to say—these days, he was a relatively healthy man. And Penelope Garner's teenage years were thankfully long past.

Yet her very existence was still causing no small amount of mischief.

Could that marriage certificate actually be authentic?

He closed the door to the suite and found the piece of paper—badly wrinkled now—on the counter in the bathroom.

Their signatures were plain. Recognizable.

Nothing about the document suggested it was a fake.

Which meant that until he could prove it was, he had to assume it was not.

He lifted his gaze to his reflection. He had more gray in his beard than he used to have. There were lines radiating from the corners of his eyes and lines in his forehead. His body had more aches and pains than he wanted to admit to.

In some circles, thirty-six wasn't all that old.

In his line of work, though, it didn't exactly make him young.

He was a member of the United States Air Force. Proud of it.

But no matter what his age, certain behaviors were frowned upon whether he was on duty or off. Finding yourself married after a night you couldn't even remember didn't exactly qualify as responsible behavior.

And now, regardless of Penny's refusal to acknowledge it, he found himself apparently married.

He pinched the bridge of his nose, wishing he could will away the throbbing pain inside his head. Instead, he turned away from the certificate and flipped on the shower before stripping off.

He wasn't particularly concerned about pleasing or not pleasing his grandmother by being late for lunch. He hadn't met her until he'd come home on leave a month ago. Until then, he'd only known the stories his father and uncle would occasionally tell about the dragon lady who'd been their mother.

Far as Quinn was concerned, the old lady was eccentric, for sure. But he had no gripe with her the way his dad did.

Of course, if Quinn hadn't let himself be talked into coming along for this damn Las Vegas trip, he wouldn't be in the situation he was in now, either. His triplet cousins—or the trips, as everyone referred to them—thought they'd maneuvered him into it. But really, he hadn't agreed until he'd learned that Penny would be there.

Still, he could just imagine the case his father would make out of the mess. David Templeton was a pediatrician. But for all of his peaceful attitude when it came to dealing with his patients and their families, he'd still find some way to lay the blame for Quinn's current predicament squarely at Vivian's door, even though Quinn was a fully capable and functioning adult.

Maybe he *was* getting soft. But he didn't want to be the cause of more dissension in his family. Not if he could help it, anyway. It wasn't as if his grandmother was going to be around forever. She'd moved to Wyoming a few years ago to make peace with her estranged family. Only she'd had a lot more success with her grandchildren than she'd had with her two sons.

He stepped under the steaming shower spray and groaned a little as the heat penetrated. It'd been three months since he and the rest of his unit had woken up to grenades exploding right outside their quarters. Three months since his life had been thrown into chaos.

Three months since his closest friend had died in the attack. Three others had been badly injured. Men, good men, who reported to Quinn. Their lives had, fortunately, moved on. Two were already headed back to the Middle East. The third was due to head out to Japan in a few weeks.

Quinn's status, however, was less certain.

Technically, his injuries were supposed to be healed. But that didn't mean he didn't still feel a gnawing ache every time he lifted his arm, courtesy of the shrapnel he'd taken during the attack. He'd spent an entire month in the hospital while the surgeons put together his shredded insides. Another month in physical therapy while the powers-that-be decided whether or not to give him the leave he'd requested.

Ultimately, he'd gotten the leave, as well as orders for ongoing therapy. The leave was supposed to last another month, if he wasn't called back up—even for light duty—because of some new disaster.

And whether his leave lasted or not, a huge question remained. What role would he be called back *to*?

Which was another reason to have a throbbing pain inside his skull.

Quinn was a PJ. A Pararescueman. It was what he loved. It was where he excelled. "These things we do, that others may live," was the PJ motto, but it was more than that for Quinn. It was a way of life. If a service member was in need of rescue on sea or on land, Quinn and others like him recovered and returned them to safety. They were commandos and they were paramedics. And they were equipped to handle anything and everything they encountered in order to complete their mission whether it was military or humanitarian in nature.

But if Quinn couldn't stand up to the physical rigors of the job, he wasn't going to be cleared for flight status. Which meant he wouldn't be going back as a PJ.

And if he couldn't go as a PJ, he wasn't sure he could stand to go back at all.

Which left him with what?

There were too many questions circling his head, not the least of which was the matter of Penny Garner.

He ducked his head beneath the shower spray, feeling the hot water sluice down his shoulders. Even after a month Stateside, he hadn't tired of the luxury of taking a shower that lasted as long as he wanted it to last.

Finally, though, aware of his grandmother's expectation, he shut off the water. He pulled on clean jeans and shirt and left his room to join his grandmother and the others for lunch.

Even before he reached the double doors of Vivian's suite, he could hear peals of laughter coming from inside.

One thing Quinn could say about the women in his family—they did know how to laugh.

He knocked on the door and a moment later, it was pulled open.

Only instead of facing his sister, Delia, or one of his cousins, it was Penny.

Like him, she'd obviously showered. Her wet hair was pulled to the back of her head into a ponytail. She'd also changed into a gray skirt that skimmed her ankles and a scoop-necked white T-shirt that lured his attention toward her lush curves.

Her eyes shied away from his as she backed out of the doorway so he could enter. "Everyone's in the dining room."

"I didn't think you were going to be here."

"Neither did I." She toyed with one of her tiny gold stud earrings. "But when Mrs. Templeton says jump, it's my job to ask how high."

"Quinn, darling." Vivian appeared in the archway leading to the dining room. She'd been widowed four times, and all of her husbands except the last had had money. Not as much as her, though, because her first husband—Quinn's grandfather—had been a steel magnate. As a result, not even a regular hotel suite was good enough for her. Nope. For his granny, it was the presidential suite. Complete with two stories, four bedrooms— three of which were going empty—a full kitchen and butler's pantry, and a formal dining room, all surrounded by an encompassing terrace if one was inclined to bake themselves in the hot Nevada sun.

"I was just getting ready to send Penny after you," Vivian said. She was petite, white-haired and typically dressed in a pale pink Chanel suit. "Come." She held out a beringed hand. "We've just been waiting for you."

He allowed her to pull him into the dining room where places had been set at one end of the long, mahogany table. His cousins were already there. But not his baby sister. "Where's Delia?"

"Still sleeping," Greer drawled, with a roll of her eyes.

"Give her a break," Maddie said calmly. "She was out all night."

"We were *all* out all night," Ali commented. She was spreading something green and obnoxious-looking across a tiny triangle of toast, and she pointed the tip of her knife at Quinn. "Except you." She waved the knife a little, taking in Penny, who'd silently come up beside Quinn. "And you, Penny. The both of you disappeared around midnight shortly after we ran into that friend of yours." She was a cop in Braden and she gave him what she obviously figured was her cop stare. But then she ruined it with a grin. "If I didn't know you better, I'd be a little suspicious what you'd gotten up to with our dear Penny."

He pulled out a chair across from Ali while Penny hurried over to the buffet that was laid out with silver serving dishes. "And what *do* you figure I was up to?" He poured himself a cup of coffee from the silver urn sitting in the center of the table.

"He was probably down in the fitness center working out like usual," Greer answered before her sister could. "As if he's not already in great shape."

"Yeah, well, great shape's not all it'll take to get me cleared for parachuting again." For that he might need a miracle. He managed a smile as he looked at their grandmother. On the bright side, at least he now knew for certain that none of his cousins had been participants in his and Penny's marital antics the night before. "Viv, how'd you sleep after all that champagne last night?"

"Like a baby. Champagne is practically mother's milk to me." She waved an indolent hand. Her attention was on Penny as she fussed with the buffet. "Penny, dear. We have you to thank for this resplendent display. Sit down and *enjoy* it."

Quinn wondered if he was the only one aware of the tight set to Penny's shoulders as she finally carried a minimally filled plate over to the table. She sat two chairs away from Quinn.

"For Delia," she murmured when he raised his eyebrows questioningly. "When she gets here."

Knowing his little sister, she'd sleep until it was time to get up and party at the next nightclub. He grabbed the handle of the fancy coffeepot and leaned across the empty chair to fill Penny's cup.

She flicked him a quick look. Murmured a thank-you.

It was obvious as hell that she wanted to be anywhere other than there.

"So how did you know Mike Lansing?" Maddie asked him. "It was so loud in the club last night, I never got that quite clear."

Quinn didn't plan to let them all know how little he remembered of the previous night and he let the name sift through his mind. He was thinking up a plausible answer when Greer took up the reins.

"They served together back in Africa," she said as she got up to refill her plate. "He was a PJ, too. Though, frankly, the guy seemed like a jerk to me. All he did was talk about himself like he was a divine gift to women." She looked at Quinn. "Fortunately, once you and Penny were gone, he didn't hang around long."

Maddie was nodding as if it all made sense.

It was beginning to make sense to Quinn, too. Thank God. Even though it was a good ten years ago since he'd met Lansing, he remembered him.

Unfortunately, he couldn't recall encountering the man at all the night before.

"Strictly speaking," he corrected, "Lansing was a CRO." He pronounced it *crow*. "Combat Rescue Officer." Which had put him ahead of Quinn—who was enlisted—in the pecking order. Until Lansing had gotten booted out for dishonorable conduct, that was.

"I don't like talking about all this military stuff," Vivian said.

Which made Quinn want to smile, because they were barely glossing the surface of military *stuff* where he was concerned.

"So, tell me. What is on everyone's schedule this afternoon?" Vivian raised her brows as she looked at all of them.

"Massage," Greer said promptly.

"Then the pool," Maddie and Ali said in unison.

Greer nodded. "That, too."

"What about you, Penny dear?"

Penny looked like she wanted to be drawn into the conversation about as much as she wanted to be thrown into the lion's den. "Whatever you need me to take care of this afternoon, Mrs. Templeton."

His grandmother made a face. "The only thing I'm doing this afternoon is resting and making a few calls."

He caught the way Penny took a closer look at Vivian. "Resting?"

"Yes." Vivian's voice was deliberately patient. "Just resting. Which means you can go about and play the same as my grandchildren. Visit the spa. The pool. Shop. Whatever you like."

"You know that I didn't bring a swimsuit." Penny didn't look at anyone as she focused on the roll that she'd been methodically shredding.

"Then go buy one, like I've been telling you to do since we got here," Vivian said firmly. "Charge it to my room. I'm sure the girls would go shopping with you." As if the matter was settled, she turned her attention to Quinn. "And you, young man? Aside from the way you seemed to loosen up last night, I haven't seen you even visit the gaming tables. You'll be the first Templeton

I've ever known who doesn't like to try his hand at a little gambling."

He shrugged. "Maybe." It would be one way to pass the rest of the day. If he hadn't had an unplanned marriage on his hands, the casino might have held a little more appeal.

"Come to the pool with us," Maddie urged. "It'll be fun."

"What kind of calls do you need to make, Vivian?" Ali started to prop her elbows on the table, then seemed to think better of it as she focused on their grandmother. She grinned. "You can rest at the pool, too, you know."

Vivian chuckled. "Well, my dear Arthur would have been the first to agree with you. But I have some business to take care of with my attorney in Pittsburgh. I'm considering selling my estate there." Her smile took in all of them. "Since I've come to the conclusion that none of my grandchildren will likely want to take up residence there, I see no reason to keep hold of the place."

Quinn had gotten accustomed to his grandmother's references to her last late husband. "Dear Arthur" had been a public school teacher. A regular guy. And even dead, he still seemed to be a guiding force in her life. So much so that to honor his memory, she'd tried mending the lifelong rifts with the family she'd had with her first husband by moving to Wyoming where everything had to be entirely backwater in comparison to the life she'd led in Pennsylvania.

"Are you sure you want to get rid of Templeton Manor for good?" Maddie looked concerned. "You lived there with Daddy's dad."

Vivian smiled faintly. "I lived there with all of my husbands. But Sawyer first of all, of course. It's the home where both of your fathers grew up." Then she made a face. "And we all know neither one of *them* wants to step foot there ever again."

"You don't know that for sure," Maddie soothed.

"Darling, you're very sweet. But I am very certain. Even though the car crash that killed their father was an accident, both Carter and David still blame me for his death. Nothing I say or do now is going to change that. But—" she placed her palms on the table beside her plate, and the diamonds on her fingers caught the light shining through the two-storied windows "—I have not given up on my grandchildren. Which is why I am so delighted that all of you were able to join me on this little jaunt to Las Vegas. I wish the rest of your siblings had been able to join us, but I'm still delighted all the same. My dear Arthur always said I'd get a kick out of this place and he was right." She stood from the table and went over to the windows. "Such ridiculous ostentation," she said, then gave them a wink. "I positively love it."

Looking at her mischievous expression, Quinn found it almost hard to believe that Vivian wasn't quite the picture of health that she appeared to be.

The reason? She called it the "little thing squatting inside my head." Quinn and everyone else in the family called it what it was. An inoperable brain tumor.

So if she wanted to treat her grandkids—those who could get away on such short notice, at least—to this impetuous, lavish trip to Las Vegas, who was he to argue?

He couldn't solve the problems between her, and his dad and uncle. But he could make sure he didn't add to the hassles between them.

Which was a good reason to get the whole marriage certificate thing with Penny squared away as soon as possible.

Almost as if she'd read his mind, Penny suddenly

stood up from the table and began clearing away her dishes.

"Penny," Vivian chided softly. "There's a butler here who takes care of that."

"I know." Penny didn't stop what she was doing. "Old habits are just too hard to break, I'm afraid." She disappeared through the connecting door into the kitchen.

"Well, I don't mind breaking habits," Greer said drily. "Someone else to clean up my dishes? I'm all for that."

Quinn tuned out his cousins' chatter as he swallowed the rest of his food, and then carried his plate and coffee into the kitchen after Penny.

She was standing at the sink with her shoulders slumped and visibly jumped when she noticed him.

"Sorry." He set his plate on the counter next to the sink. Didn't mean to startle you."

"You didn't."

It was such an obvious lie, he let it go unchallenged.

"We'll get it worked out, Penny."

Her jaw shifted from side to side. "I don't want to talk about it here."

"I have the feeling you don't want to talk about it anywhere."

She shot him a pained look.

He sighed and looked over his shoulder through to the dining room. His cousins and grandmother were still sitting at the long table. "The certificate's signed by an officiant. I'm going to check it out this afternoon. See what I can learn." He considered asking if she wanted to accompany him but decided not to. If she didn't want to discuss it, he doubted she'd want to traipse around with him looking into it.

"We were drunk. Obviously." Her voice was low.

"There's no other explanation. It's probably not even legal."

He wasn't going to debate the matter when he didn't know the legalities, either. "I'll let you know what I find out."

Her long lashes swept down, hiding her vividly blue eyes again. She nodded and turned on the faucet to rinse another plate before leaning over to place it inside the built-in dishwasher.

There didn't seem much point hanging there. Particularly when the only thing his eyes wanted to do was linger on the creamy skin exposed below her T-shirt when she'd leaned over.

His fingers twitched slightly, tingling. He knew exactly how her smooth, supple skin felt.

He also knew exactly how her skin tasted. It was there inside his memory, bright and vivid, even though he didn't specifically recall anything besides waking up with his arms full of her warm body.

"Quinn!"

He dragged his mind into the present when he heard his name being called from the other room.

Penny had straightened and was rinsing another dish beneath the faucet. Shoulders hunched. Eyes averted.

He curled his fingers against his palms but the prickling sensation didn't go away.

"Quinn!" Typically impatient, Ali came to the kitchen doorway. "Have beans in your ears? I've been calling you."

He ignored her. "We'll get it worked out, Penny," he said again in a low voice, before turning to face his cousin. "*What*?"

Ali's gaze was flipping from him to Penny and back to him again. Her cop's mind was undoubtedly conjecturing. "Nothing," she said after a moment. "Nothing at all." Smiling faintly, she turned and left the room.

"And *that's* why I didn't want to talk about it here," Penny muttered behind him.

He glanced at her. "You going to be one of those wives who always has to be right?"

She flushed. Gave him a look fit to do more damage than the grenades had done. "I am *not* your wife," she muttered between her teeth.

"For both our sakes, darlin', I hope you're right."

Chapter Three

The clerk at the county marriage bureau was polite, friendly and adamant.

It was entirely likely that Penny Garner really was his wife.

And the pain inside Quinn's head rose to a new level.

"The officiant—" the clerk deciphered the signature on the marriage certificate "—Marvin Morales, has ten days to file your certificate. We often get them within a few days of the wedding, though. Once the marriage is recorded, a certified copy is typically available after a day or so." She handed him back his crumpled paper. She'd already told him it was merely his keepsake certificate versus the official document. If she had any personal opinion about the state of the piece of paper, she kept it to herself. "You can get certified copies in person, via regular mail or order them online."

Even though it was Sunday afternoon, there was a

long line of people waiting behind him for their turn at the counter.

The Las Vegas wedding business was clearly in fine form.

"And this Morales guy. He's legit?"

She turned to her computer and tapped on the keys. "Certainly is," she assured. "I'm not showing any address or organizational affiliation for him, though."

That didn't sound overly legitimate to him. "Is that normal?"

"It's a little unusual, but not unheard of." She smiled. "Is there anything else I can help you with, Mr. Templeton?"

Right next to his elbow a large sign was posted, indicating the bureau would not issue marriage licenses to individuals who were clearly intoxicated. He nodded toward it. "You really enforce that?"

For the first time the clerk looked a little miffed. "Of course, sir. We take our responsibilities here quite seriously."

"I'm sure you do." He folded the certificate. "I appreciate your time."

"Certainly. I wish you and your bride every happiness."

He managed a smile as he turned away from the counter. He had barely vacated the spot when it was replaced by a young couple who were practically bouncing out of their shoes with excitement.

Outside the building, the sun was bright and hot. A good twenty-five degrees hotter than it was back in Wyoming. He didn't particularly mind the heat, though. He'd served all over the world. He was used to temperature extremes.

He wound his way through the wedding-chapel vendors hawking their services outside the building and even though there were plenty of cabs he could have hailed, he walked back to the hotel.

The moment he entered, cold air and piped music engulfed him. If he went one direction, he could head toward his hotel suite. If he headed the opposite direction, he'd end up in one of the endless casinos. Another direction and it was one of the hotel's several pools.

He wasn't one for indecision, but he just stood there on the sea of gleaming marble tile, feeling the artificially cooled air blowing down over his head while he ran his thumb along the folded edges of the marriage certificate.

"Looks like you survived the fun last night, Sarge."

At the greeting, Quinn looked up to see Mike Lansing a few feet away. Even if the trips hadn't mentioned him from the night before, Quinn still would have recognized the other man. He had one arm looped over the shoulders of a bored-looking blonde and held a drink in his other hand.

"I did." Quinn slid the folded square in his back pocket. "You?"

The blonde pursed her lips and looked up at Mike. "Are we going to the shops or not?"

Mike pulled out a wad of cash and pushed it into her hand. "You go, baby. I'm gonna grab another drink with my old buddy, here."

The woman's boredom visibly brightened as she tucked the money down her bra. She pulled Mike's head down and gave him a noisy kiss. "See you later in the room." Even though her voice was loaded with innuendo, she still ran her eyes up and down Quinn when she turned and walked away.

"Nice girl," Quinn commented blandly.

Mike laughed. "Better be, considering how much she's costing me."

Since that could be taken a couple of ways, Quinn refrained from comment.

"C'mon." Mike gestured with his half-full glass. "There's a sweet little cocktail waitress I've been eyeing."

"What about Miss Shopper?"

Mike just grinned and led the way toward the casino. "What about her?"

Quinn shook his head and followed. He didn't care at all about Mike in a general sense, but the guy *had* evidently been around the night before. Quinn was willing to put up with most anything if it helped jog his memory of what had occurred.

They went straight to the lounge and had barely settled at one of the high-tops before a shapely redhead in a short black dress came over to take their orders. Mike ordered another whiskey and the waitress turned her smile toward Quinn. "And for you, sir?"

"Ginger ale."

Mike gave him a look. "Dude."

"Ginger ale," Quinn repeated drily to the waitress.

She smiled at him, ignored the leer in Mike's eyes and walked away.

"Talk about a fine-looking pair of legs," Mike murmured, watching her go. "Not as good as those hot cousins of yours, but still fine."

Quinn's jaw tightened. "Can't remember if you said last night what you're doing here in Vegas."

Mike laughed as if it was uproariously funny. He clapped Quinn on the shoulder. "I'll bet you can't remember." He sat back and finished off his drink just in time to exchange it for the fresh one the redhead returned with. "Thanks, sweetheart. What time you get off work?"

"Soon as my husband picks up our twin babies," she replied with a sweet smile. She set Quinn's glass of soda on a round coaster. "I'll be back to check on you boys."

"Babies." Mike shuddered. "God forbid. Least we've both been smart enough to avoid that nightmare. Remember Rollie? The way his old lady was always harping on him? Deployments keeping him away from her and those kids she kept poppin' out? Ask me, I bet more than one of them wasn't even Rollie's. Always said the smartest guys are the ones who don't bother putting a ring on it."

Quinn didn't entirely disagree. The divorce rate among special operators was astronomically high. He also knew many of the guys kept trying anyway. Maybe it was the hope to keep something normal in a world that was anything but normal.

Some succeeded.

More didn't.

For his part, Quinn had always figured that if he'd ever met a woman he wanted to marry, he'd expect to put as much commitment into that marriage as he had into his career.

He'd just never met a woman that special.

The folded marriage certificate inside his pocket felt like it was burning a tattoo into his butt.

He shifted. "You got out a long time ago," he reminded Mike, skirting the actual facts of the guy's discharge. "What have you been doing since?"

"Contract work." Mike grinned. "Money is really good, dude. Still get to make bad guys dead, but the bennies are a lot better than Uncle Sam ever coughed up. You decide you want to make some real dough, say the word. You think the uniform is a chick magnet, you should see what a bankroll can do. I'll make some introductions."

"If money had ever been my goal, I'd have become

an officer like you were," Quinn drawled. His first impressions of Mike Lansing had held up over the years. The hot five-mile walk from the marriage bureau building hadn't made him want a shower as badly as sitting there with Mike did.

Mike laughed again. "You're a master sergeant now. Good reason to feel uptight right there. Must suck being stuck running the action from the ground."

Quinn hadn't been stuck running things from the ground, but it was a definite possibility facing him. Even though every single member of the combat rescue team was valuable, running things from the ground wasn't a role he relished. He'd spent too long in the action. Too long as a team leader.

"Just say the word and I'll hook you up with another hit that'll have you loosening up again in no time." Mike grinned, mimicking dropping something into his drink.

His attention abruptly targeted on Mike. "Another hit. Of *what*?"

"A little something I keep handy."

Quinn's fists curled. "Exactly what little something?"

"Nothing that'll pop in a blood test," Mike assured, as if that made everything all right. "Just an herbal cocktail I learned about last time I was in India. Makes life a little…brighter. Your sister thought it was pretty hilarious. She switched drinks with yours—" He broke off when Quinn stood and started walking away. "Hey, Sarge. Where're you going?"

Anywhere other than there.

Quinn didn't stop. Didn't even bother looking back. If he did, he was afraid of what he'd do to the other man.

Mike was a worm. Always had been and it seemed nothing in the intervening decade had changed.

But the last thing Quinn needed was to be caught

grinding his fist into a worm's face. He didn't need an assault charge haunting him, no matter how well deserved his actions felt.

He strode through the casino until he located the elevators and went up to Delia's hotel suite. Banged on the door. "Delia!"

Relief hit him when she finally yanked open the door. She was clearly dressed for the swimming pool in a bikini and a flimsy cover-up that didn't cover up a damn thing. "What are you doing here?"

"Looking for you, obviously." He sounded annoyed and didn't care. Because he was annoyed. Not only at Mike's stunt, but also with her. "What the hell are you walking around like that for? You're practically naked."

Her eyebrows shot up and she propped her hand on her hip. She was dark-haired like him but that was about the end of the similarities. "I'm a long way from naked *and* I'm not exactly sixteen anymore, so can the protective growl!"

He would always feel protective where Delia was concerned. Mostly because she was the baby of his family. But also—and he ordinarily said it with love—she was kind of a ditz.

Their father was a pediatrician. Their mother was a retired psychologist. Their other sister, Grace, was doing her residency at Duke. Much to his father's chagrin at the time, Quinn hadn't taken the educational route, but he'd still made a career out of his military service and gotten a hell of a lot of education along the way.

Delia, though? She seemed entirely happy coasting through life, never settling on anything or anyone for any length of time.

"Did you see Lansing doctor my drink last night?"

She pursed her lips. "Maybe."

God help him. He wanted to shake her. "Yes or no?"

"Good grief, Quinn. Keep your shorts on." She picked up an oversize shoulder bag sitting on a chair. A floppy hat and a rolled towel were sticking out of it. "Of course I saw. He put some drops in Penny's drink, too."

"And you switched drinks."

"So?"

He wanted to yell at her. But Delia never responded well to shouting. She just crumpled up in tears and shut down. "Are you crazy? I suppose you just drank it, too. Did he spike anyone else's?"

She glared. "No, I did not drink it," she snapped. "I dumped them both in a plant by the table! And no, I didn't see him do anything else."

"Did it occur to you to say anything? He could have been putting *anything* in our drinks. I can't even remember coming back to the hotel last night." But that wasn't entirely accurate, either. Because already he had images hovering on the edges of his pain-addled brain. Vivid city lights. Penny's blue gaze. A glossy limousine interior...

"When was I supposed to tell you, Quinn? When you were busy feeling up Penny on the dance floor? Besides, the guy was all hands! By the time I got *that* dealt with, you and Penny had already disappeared!"

"You could have found a way," he said through his teeth. "You have no idea what a mess this has caused."

"Well?" She spread her hands, clearly waiting. "What mess?"

He clenched his jaw, remembering his promise to Penny. "Lansing's been a lost cause for ten years. But you're my sister. You're twenty-seven years old. You see something wrong, you *speak up!*"

"At least *I* was more aware of what was going on than you were." She snatched a small vial from her pool bag and thrust it at him. "I stole it from his jacket while he was trying to stick his tongue down my throat. You're *welcome*."

He exhaled roughly, rubbing his hand down his face as he swore. At her. At Lansing. At the fact that he'd found himself married to a woman who was more appalled at the idea than he was. But mostly at himself. Because Delia was right. If he'd been more aware, none of this would have happened. "Thank you," he muttered.

Delia sniffed, clearly unimpressed as she shoved past him with her pool bag and strode away.

"Perfect." He opened the nearly empty vial and took a sniff, which told him nothing. He twisted the cap back in place and pocketed it.

He realized he didn't know the number of Penny's room as he headed toward the elevator. He used the house phone to call the front desk and, thanks to the beauty of dropping his granny's name, received the information he needed.

He took the elevator down to Penny's floor and knocked on the door. Given the way the day had gone so far, he didn't expect her to be there, so when the door opened a second later, he couldn't hide his surprise.

At least that was the excuse he used while he adjusted to the sight of her. She was wearing a black swimsuit with an opaque black scarf tied around her hips. The sleek one-piece was a lot less revealing than Delia's bikini had been, but disturbed him a hell of a lot more.

It wasn't easy to believe he'd wedded Penny, but it was all too easy to understand why he'd bedded her.

No amount of artificial stimulants needed on that score.

"I see you went shopping for a swimsuit."

Her hair was still pulled back in a ponytail—dry

now—and she had a pair of sunglasses hiding her eyes.
"Yes."

"Can I come in?"

She hesitated.

He led with what he considered the most critical info.
"The guy Maddie mentioned at lunch—Lansing. He
drugged our drinks last night."

Her lips parted. She slowly pushed her sunglasses onto
the top of her head.

"With what?" She backed away, pulling the door open
wider so he could enter.

Her hotel room was just a regular hotel room. Nice,
yeah. But nothing at all like the fancy-dancy suites the
rest of them had. It was also neat as a pin. The bed perfectly made because she hadn't even spent the last night
in it. "Supposedly it's some herbal crap." He showed
her the vial.

She paled. "What kind of herbal crap?"

I don't know, but I know someone who can test it. He
pushed the vial in his pocket again and put his hand on
her forehead. The skin was cool. Velvety smooth. "How
are you feeling? A headache? Any nausea? Problems
breathing?"

She shook her head, pulling away from his touch. "No.
Well, a headache. But I just attributed that to…you know."
She turned away from him.

The back straps of her swimsuit were comprised of an
intriguing series of strings crisscrossing over the small
of her spine in a way that only emphasized her hour-
glass figure. And even though he couldn't see beneath
the scarf, he had no problem imagining her long legs and
curvy butt being shown off to perfection…

He cleared his throat and looked away.

She was pacing in the space between the bed and the

window. "We've all heard to watch out for that sort of thing, but to have it actually happen—" She plopped on the side of the bed. "Has this happened to you before?"

He sighed and went to sit beside her. "No." He folded her hand in his. "I'm sorry."

"Because your friend is an ass?"

"He was kicked out of the service ten years ago. And he was never my friend. But yeah."

She looked at him. Her brows were pulled together over those oddly luminous eyes. "You didn't know. None of us knew."

"Except Delia." He let go of her hand, pushing off the bed. "She saw him do it. And if she'd *said* something—" he yanked the marriage certificate out of his back pocket and tossed it on the bed beside her "—maybe we wouldn't have that to deal with."

She got off the bed as if she didn't want to be any-where near the certificate. "You didn't tell her, did you?"

"That's what you're worried about? No, I didn't tell her. I told you I wouldn't say anything to anyone yet and I haven't." He gestured at the paper. "The guy who signed it is registered with the county to perform marriages. I'll have to keep checking back to get proof it's legal, but we'll know that within ten days. That's how long he has to file the paperwork."

"Ten days!"

"Could be sooner." He told her everything the mar-riage bureau employee had told him.

"So we were lucid enough to apply for a marriage li-cense. Presumably get through a ceremony of some sort and sign our names on the marriage certificate. Then pass out in bed. It doesn't mean we can't get an annulment." Her cheeks were red. "We don't know that…that…any-thing physical happened."

"Don't pretend you're that naive. I can't see us being in bed together and not *being* in bed together." The way they'd woken all tangled together was proof enough for him. He'd been hard as a rock and she'd been warm and wet.

She'd pressed her hands over her ears and was shaking her head. "I'm not listening."

He went over to her and gently wrapped his fingers around her wrists. Her pulse rate was off the charts. "Like it or not, Penny, it's a given that you and I consummated whatever vows we exchanged." He exhaled heavily and admitted the worst. "But I can't even be certain that you were willing!"

Her lips parted. She swallowed. "Quinn—"

He let her go and shoved his hand through his hair. "If you want go to the hospital, I can take you. Or arrange for someone else to, if you're more comfortable that way." His voice was gruff. The thought that he might have coerced her was nauseating. "You can get an exam. If you were forced —"

"Oh my God!" She looked horrified. "I don't need an exam to prove what I already know. You were just as much a victim of this as I was. Maybe you were the one who wasn't, you know...on board." Her cheeks turned red. "That'd be more in line with our history."

"Trust me." His voice was dark. "I would've been more than willing back then if you'd have been legal. And now—" He broke off because her face was nearly scarlet now. He exhaled. "You're a beautiful woman, Penny. Let's just leave it at that."

She cleared her throat, not looking at him. "And you're a handsome man." The words seemed to come reluctantly. "Anyway, it's all moot," she continued abruptly. "I don't care what sort of influence you were under. You'd never do something against a woman's will. You wouldn't even be worried if not for what that scum of a man did. So just stop thinking about it and talking about…about tests and stuff."

His chest felt tight. Trust like that was more than a little humbling. And he still wasn't sure it was merited. How could he ever be truly sure?

"Promise me, Quinn."

It was the second promise she'd asked of him that day. "Fine."

Fortunately, she accepted the answer. She put a few paces between them, busying herself with retying the knot in the silky scarf. "And maybe we didn't. It's *possible*," she insisted at his look. "Maybe we both just passed out before we could—you know."

"Have sex?"

"Yes." Obviously, the very idea of it embarrassed her. "Regardless, we're the only ones who would know. And if we say we didn't…consummate things, we could still get an annulment."

"You mean lie."

"It's not a lie if there's any room for doubt."

He made a face and she huffed. "Neither one of us wants to be married to the other. This is just one big fiasco from start to finish. And the only way to rectify it—if there's anything to actually rectify—is to get an annulment. Everything'll be right back to normal."

"You're forgetting one thing."

She raised her brows, waiting.

"When we had sex—"

"*If* we had sex."

"When we had sex," he repeated over her interruption, "we didn't use anything." No condom. No condom wrapper. No evidence of any sort of protection had been in his hotel suite. "Now, I've had every medical test known to man over the past few months. You don't have to worry about catching anything from me. I'm assuming you've always been careful in the past?"

Her cheeks had gone red again. After a moment she gave a stiff nod.

"Then there's just one question left. Are you on birth control?"

Chapter Four

Quinn's words jangled inside Penny's mind.

He was standing there, annoyingly handsome and militarily straight, waiting for an answer.

She wanted to ask him if they hadn't already had enough blows for one day.

She was still grappling with the notion that some idiot had spiked their drinks. The only thing gained by knowing that fact was that they now had an explanation for ending up in Quinn's hotel suite the way they had. They had an explanation for not being able to remember any of it. She already knew Quinn had an overdeveloped sense of responsibility. If he learned she'd also been a virgin—

"Penny?" Quinn took a step toward her. His eyebrows were like straight slashes above his level brown eyes. "Are you on birth control or not?"

"I don't really think that's any of your business," she said evasively.

His eyebrows shot up. "Until I know otherwise, you're my wife. I think that *does* make it my business. So are you on the pill? Implant? Anything?"

"Mmm-hmm." She managed a nod, trying valiantly to pretend her neck wasn't getting hot.

His eyes narrowed. "You're lying."

The heat spread up her jaw and into her cheeks. Her forehead. Until her entire head felt like it might well be smoking. "Why would I lie about that?"

He suddenly leaned back against the dresser in front of the bed and folded his arms across his wide chest. "I don't know," he said calmly. "Why are you?"

She'd been a better liar when she'd been ten than she was now.

She turned her back on him and went over to look out the window. Unlike his suite with that stellar city view and balcony, her room looked out over a roof and a bunch of mechanical equipment. There was one window. No balcony. And it was still costing Mrs. Templeton over four hundred dollars a night.

"No, I'm not on the pill," she admitted flatly. "There's nobody in my life. Hasn't been for a while." She wasn't going to tell him that there'd never been anyone. Not that way. She and her fiancé, Andy, had been foster kids living in the same foster home. They'd never chanced it, knowing that they'd be separated in a nanosecond if they were caught doing anything improper. Then he'd graduated from high school, announced to their foster parents during his graduation party that they were engaged, and he'd headed to boot camp a day later, leaving Penny behind to finish high school.

Quinn's silence penetrated her memories and she looked over her shoulder at him. "*What?*"

"You're not on anything?"

She shook her head.

He closed his eyes and rubbed his fingertips against his temples. "So you could be pregnant. On top of everything else."

"What? No!"

He gave her a look. "I don't have to spell out the details of unprotected sex, do I?"

She made a face. "Obviously not."

"Then you know there's a chance just as well as I do." He inhaled deeply, then straightened once more. "Which means nothing's happening about *anything* until we know one way or the other."

She couldn't remember making love. She darn shooting couldn't imagine having conceived a baby with him. She and Andy had talked about having a half-dozen kids. About having the kind of real family that neither one of them had grown up with.

Her throat felt tight. "I can't talk about this anymore." She hurried past him and yanked open the room door. "I need you to go."

"Penny."

She stared hard at the gold patterned carpet beneath her sandals, willing away the tears that burned behind her eyes. "Please, Quinn. Not now." Not *ever*, if she was lucky.

She heard the impatience in his sigh as he came over to the door. But there was no hint of impatience at all in the way he touched her shoulder. And no matter how badly she wanted to ignore him, she couldn't help looking up at him.

For a man who could look as fierce as he could look, he also had an unsettling capacity for showing extreme gentleness.

And she felt shaky because of it.

"Whatever happens, whatever we learn, we will work it out together. All right?"

Her teeth were practically gnawing a chunk out of the inside of her cheek. "I'm not your responsibility, Quinn."

"Well, now, I'm going to have to disagree, since you seem to be my wife."

"An unintentional one."

"Doesn't make it any less real as far as I'm concerned. And as such, you are my responsibility."

"Doesn't that make you my responsibility, as well?"

His thumb rubbed her bare shoulder before falling away. "You can handle it. You handle Vivian, after all. And she's a lot more to take on than me."

Despite everything, Penny felt a tearful laugh catch in her throat. "I'd just gotten off the phone with her when you knocked on my door." Her hand felt sweaty on the door handle.

"How'd you end up working for her anyway? You get tired of working for my dad or something? You worked for him a long time."

"Ten years," she murmured. So long that she'd even become Dr. Templeton's office manager. "I met Mrs. Templeton when she came to see your dad at his office last summer."

"Bet that went well." His voice was dry.

She nodded. "They had a shouting match. About what you'd expect. Before she left, she told me that I looked intelligent enough if not for the fact that I worked for her son."

"Nice."

"I think the only reason she started calling me to come work for her as her assistant was because she knew it annoyed your father." She hesitated because she wasn't sure Dr. T would appreciate her sharing the truth, even with his own son. "Eventually, she offered double my salary. Your dad said I should take it. I started working for her shortly before last Christmas."

"Just like that. Ten years of loyalty tossed aside for a few dollars more?"

The accusation accomplished what nothing else did. It dried up the knot of tears threatening to break loose inside her.

"He said I should take it for the money, and then he asked me to keep my eye on her for him. No matter what he says about not caring about your grandmother, your dad *does* care. Very much. And because I care about Dr. Templeton, I did what he asked."

"You did what my son asked, dear?"

Penny caught her breath and looked out the door she was holding open to see Vivian standing a few feet away in the hall.

How much had she heard?

Vivian's carefully penciled eyebrows went up as she approached. "Well?"

Penny couldn't seem to form an answer to save her life. She looked up at Quinn. He looked surprised, but definitely wasn't at a loss.

"She told him she'd keep an eye on me while we were here in Vegas," he lied easily. "You know what Dad's like."

"Overprotective," Vivian said crisply. "When it comes to my possible bad influence." Her bright gaze was running back and forth between Penny's face and her grandson's. "Well, I can't say that's much of a surprise." She brushed her hand down the lapel of her chenille jacket as if she were brushing away the thought. "Is that what the two of you are doing together in your room, Penny? Looking after my grandson?"

Penny's face went hot.

Which seemed to be exactly the response that Vivian was looking for, because the elderly woman gave a faint smile and a sage-looking nod.

If Quinn noticed, he ignored it. "What're you doing slumming on the fifth floor anyway, Vivian?"

"Now you sound like dear Arthur. He had that attitude about me when we first met."

"You cured him of it?" Quinn's voice was wry.

"He cured *me* of it," Vivian said simply. "Now, Penny dear. I came down to tell you that we're starting a new project."

Wariness coursed through her. Vivian's latest project had been planning this Las Vegas jaunt.

And look where *that* had landed them.

"What project is that, Mrs. Templeton?"

"I've decided to run for the open seat on the town council."

Penny blinked. She wasn't sure she'd heard right. "Weaver's town council?"

"Well, not Las Vegas's town council," Vivian said humorously. "Now, the vote isn't until September, which gives us a little over six weeks to mount my campaign."

"I didn't know you were interested in politics."

"Oh." Vivian looked annoyed. "I'm not. But *somebody* needs to run against that coot, Squire Clay, and since nobody else in town has stepped up to do it, I will. I'm hardly afraid of an old cattle rancher, even if he does think he owns the entire town. Do you know that he actually tried to keep me from building my house where I wanted it? Said I was impinging on the natural view from the town. You can't even *see* my house from the edge of town."

Penny had never met Squire Clay, herself, though she'd

certainly heard the man's name. The Clay family owned one of the largest cattle ranches in the state and as far as she knew, they formed a good portion of the very backbone of Weaver. The Clays were also relatives of the Templetons, though that was a recent revelation Vivian had admitted to only after she'd moved to Weaver from Pittsburgh.

"Vivian," Quinn offered reasonably, "I've heard you and Clay aren't the best of friends, but—"

"We're not even the best of enemies." Vivian cut off Quinn. "He's as bad as my two sons when it comes to holding old grudges. I can't imagine how any sister of my Sawyer—illegitimate or otherwise—could have had the bad taste to marry a man like Squire. He was a boor sixty years ago and nothing has changed in the years since. It's amazing to me that he actually found another woman willing to marry him after Sarah died." She focused on Penny again. "So, the first order of business is to make sure my name is filed right away as a candidate. I want you to take care of that even before we leave for home. All right?"

"Of course." Penny had no clue whatsoever what was involved, but she knew how to pick up a phone and ask questions.

"Very good." Vivian smiled, running her gaze approvingly over the bathing suit that Penny had reluctantly purchased at her boss's insistence. "Now, run along, you two. Get to the pool. The manager here has invited me to join him for dinner, so you'll be on your own this evening. We'll all have breakfast in my suite before we check out of the hotel, so I'd appreciate you arranging that, Penny. Quinn, make sure Delia drags herself to breakfast, also. Until then, I trust you'll find something to entertain yourselves." Smiling slightly, she turned on her heel and strode away.

Neither Penny nor Quinn spoke until the old woman was out of sight.

"So that tumor is making her crazy now," he finally said.

"She's definitely not crazy."

He was silent for a moment. A moment in which she became painfully aware of the warmth of his shoulder where it brushed against hers.

"My old man really asked you to keep an eye on her?"

She moistened her lips. Little prickles of sensation were springing to life beneath her skin. "He really asked me." If Quinn would move even an inch, she could have slid past him back into the safety of her hotel room instead of standing there in the opened doorway.

But he wasn't moving.

Not even an inch.

She tugged at the knot on her scarf, tightening the slick fabric once more. Ali had been the one to insist the bathing suit was perfect. But Maddie had tossed in the scarf, obviously understanding that Penny didn't feel comfortable parading around in a suit that left so much of her butt exposed.

"He's suspicious of her. That's why he wants you watching her."

It was easier to focus on her impatience than the fact that her stupid hormones were acting up. She refused to believe that simply standing near Quinn was turning her on.

"Your father wants me to keep an eye on her *health*. He gave me a whole list of things to watch out for. None of which I have seen in the past eight months, mind you. You might as well believe me, because I have no reason to make it up." She braced herself and brushed past him once and for all, crossing the entire width of the hotel room just to put some space between them.

The marriage certificate was still lying on the bed where he'd left it.

She turned her back on it and looked out at the oh-so-enticing roof view. The shiver dancing up and down her spine had her imagining his intense gaze centered right between her shoulder blades.

"You're right," he said quietly.

Then she heard the door close softly and her pulse ratcheted into high gear.

She swallowed and moistened her lips, certain beyond certainty that he was silently making his way across the plush carpet toward her.

Her knees felt weak. She pressed her forehead against the windowpane.

Considering the blazing sunshine, the glass ought to have felt at least warm. But it was cool. Thickly insulated against the elements.

It was only inside her belly that she felt hot.

She closed her eyes. "Quinn. I don't want to make this situation more complicated than it already is."

He didn't answer.

She finally turned to look his way.

The hotel room was empty.

He'd closed the door all right. But after leaving.

Her breath oozed out shakily and she pressed her hand to her pounding chest and sank down onto the bed.

Vivian Templeton wasn't crazy.

But Penny was more than a little afraid that *she* was.

She could feel the marriage certificate crumpled beneath her hip and she tugged it free and tossed it onto the floor where she couldn't see or feel it. Then she grabbed the bed pillow and buried her face in it, wishing she couldn't feel anything at all.

She'd lost everything that mattered in her life the day that Andy had died. The only thing that had kept her from wanting to crawl into the box in which they'd sent him back to her, had been Dr. Templeton's unceasing nagging for her to show up every day at work. He'd given her work. He'd gotten her to take college classes online.

She'd kept on living. She'd kept on breathing.

But she'd stopped feeling.

Until today.

Until she'd wakened in Quinn Templeton's arms.

It was a painful realization. Knowing that she hadn't lost the capacity to feel anything at all. Much less that it would be because of someone like Quinn.

She couldn't have chosen someone more unsuitable if she'd tried.

Housekeeping had visited his suite by the time Quinn let himself back into the room after leaving Penny's.

His head was still pounding like a jackhammer and he opened the minibar and popped open a can of cola. It didn't matter to him that it wasn't cold. He needed caffeine and he drank it straight down.

Then he crumpled the can and pitched it into the trash and chased the soda with a full bottle of water.

Then he fell back on the bed and stared at the ceiling.

The ache in his side was nothing compared to the ache in his head. But that one would abate. It was only a matter of time.

The one in his side?

He wasn't so sure about that one.

He dropped one arm over his face. But every time he closed his eyes, he saw Penny.

The situation would be a helluva lot easier if he wasn't so attracted to her.

It wasn't just physically, though she'd always been a looker.

It was something inside that head of hers that he couldn't get out of *his* head. Something deep behind her brilliantly blue eyes.

The phone rang, jangling through his thoughts.

He considered letting it go, but habits died too hard for a soldier and he rolled over and snatched it off the hook. "Templeton."

"Are you coming to the pool or not?" It was Greer. Behind her was the sound of music and voices and laughter. "We've been saving a lounge chair for you and we're getting some seriously dirty looks."

Noise was exactly what he didn't want.

But he wasn't thrilled being stuck with his own thoughts, either.

Is Penny there?

He wanted to ask but didn't.

There'd already been too many knowing looks tossed around from his family when it came to him and Penny, and he wasn't going to add fuel to that particular fire. "Give up the chair," he advised. "I'm going to the fitness center."

"He's going to work out," he heard her tell someone. "You just won me twenty bucks, cuz," she told him with a laugh. Then she hung up.

"Glad to be of service," he murmured and dropped the phone back on the cradle.

Then he rolled off the bed and headed into the bathroom, muttering a curse as his stiff muscles protested.

He forgot that annoyance, though, when he noticed

the shining wedding band tucked against the zipper of his shaving kit.

He looped the ring over his little finger. It didn't even pass his first knuckle as he studied it. The channel-set diamonds caught the light.

Disjointed puzzle pieces floated inside his memory. They were so close he could almost put his finger on them. Almost fit them into place.

But even if he never could put them together, nothing was changed.

He'd married Penny Garner.

As had been the case when they'd flown *to* Las Vegas, Vivian and her crew flew back to Wyoming in a private, chartered jet.

Vivian kept Penny occupied well enough. She spent half the flight brainstorming her next trip with her grandchildren, and the other half strategizing her new town council campaign. Which left Penny with several pages of notes as she'd scrambled to keep up with the woman's rapid ideas.

It was a relief when they finally landed at Braden's bare-bones airport, which consisted of two runways, a hangar and a flight service station. Penny tipped the flight crew while the others got off the plane, then hurried after them to pile into Vivian's outrageously out-of-place Rolls Royce that had been parked in the dirt parking lot for the past few days. With Quinn behind the wheel, they dropped off his cousins first at their place, then Delia at her apartment.

Then it was time to let off Quinn.

Instead of his parents' place, Quinn drove to a house that Penny wasn't familiar with and parked on the street at the curb. She got out of the backseat where she'd been riding, prepared to take his place behind the wheel.

It was to everyone's benefit that Vivian be kept from driving as much as possible.

It wasn't that she was incapable. But Vivian had a tendency to jump curbs and run over trash cans. She hadn't ever hit anything more serious, and everyone wanted to keep it that way.

He'd opened the trunk to remove his duffel bag and he stepped in her path when she was rounding the back of the luxury vehicle. The trunk lid wasn't tall enough to hide them from view of Vivian still in the vehicle, and Penny gave him a wary look.

"What's your address?" His voice was low.

There was no point in not telling him. He would be able to get it from any number of people if he asked. She reeled it off and he nodded before handing her a folded envelope.

"What's that?"

"Your wedding ring."

She paled, remembering the diamond band she'd yanked off her finger the day before. "I don't want it." She shoved the envelope into the mesh pocket on the side of his duffel.

His lips thinned. "You think I do?" He shut the trunk.

He walked back to the driver's door and waited until Penny had gotten inside before shutting the door.

Then he leaned down through the open window and Penny felt her breath catching in her chest.

But all he did was tell her to drive safely, before looking past her to his grandmother. "Vivian, it's been a memorable trip."

"Yes, it has." His grandmother smiled benignly. "You

come and see me again before you go back to duty. That's an order."

His smile was faint but he nodded. "Yes, ma'am."

Then his eyes met Penny's briefly before he straightened and walked toward the house, the long strap of the duffel bag hitched easily over his shoulder.

"He reminds me so much of Sawyer," Vivian murmured. "I so wish he weren't in such a dangerous profession."

"Did your first husband serve in the military?" She realized she still didn't know what exactly Quinn did for the air force. The term PJ meant nothing to her, unless it was a nickname for *pajamas*.

Something that Quinn hadn't been wearing when she'd wakened in his bed.

Vivian's voice broke into that particularly vivid memory. "Sawyer's father's money bought him out of it. Then our money bought David and Carter out of it." Her smile turned sad for a moment.

Then her shoulders lifted and fell in a deep breath and she patted Penny's hand with her heavily jeweled fingers. "Let's go home, dear. One adventure is done, but we've got lots of work ahead of us for the next."

Penny adjusted the seat closer after Quinn's longer legs and put the car carefully in gear before driving away from the house.

In the rearview mirror, though, she could see Quinn standing on his porch, watching them go.

And she knew the *adventure* with him had a long way to go before Penny would be able to consider it done.

Chapter Five

"What do you think about this?" Penny turned the computer screen toward Vivian. On it was a display of the "Templeton for Town Council" campaign poster Penny had been laboring over.

To say she wasn't an expert when it came to campaign materials was an understatement. But she'd found a bunch of images on the internet and had been running her version of them past her boss all morning.

Vivian was sitting on her favored settee in her office. From its position, she had a view of the lushly landscaped grounds behind her newly built mansion, and now she propped her glasses on her nose and peered over to where Penny was sitting at the gigantic desk. "That looks fine, dear." She squinted a little, running her hand up and down the heavy strand of pearls draped around her neck. "But no purple in the printing. Perhaps blue instead. Royal blue, though. No navy. It's positively boring." She slid off her glasses and turned to study the landscaping once again. "What happened between you and Quinn last weekend?"

On the outside, Penny went stock-still.

On the inside, however, her nerves went into overdrive.

"I'm not sure what you mean." She carefully turned the computer screen back to face her, but she couldn't even begin to touch the keyboard. Not with the way her fingers were shaking.

They'd returned to Wyoming the afternoon before.

And in the twenty-four hours since, Penny had been in an agony of waiting for Quinn to contact her. There was no doubt that he would.

As much as she wanted to buy into the entire "what happens in Vegas stays in Vegas," she couldn't. Most particularly because she knew *he* couldn't.

Given the choice, she'd just go along pretending as if nothing had ever happened there. It wasn't as if she intended to marry another person for real, after all.

Marriage and family?

If Andy's death hadn't already proven to her, once and for all, that she was not destined for such things, then the disastrous way she'd ended up in Quinn's hotel suite had provided a pretty good capper.

Vivian propped her glasses on her nose again, but evidently, only so that she could give Penny a long look over the top of the narrow, silver frames. "Aside from the guilty look on your face when I found you together in your hotel room, and the even guiltier look on your face now, you mean?" She slid off her glasses again and gestured with them toward the tall, arched windows that lined the wall in front of her settee. "How about the fact

that Quinn is outside right now, mulching the new spruce
trees?"

From overdrive to hyperdrive.

Before Penny could stop herself, she got up from the
desk and walked around to see out the windows from
Vivian's perspective. The grounds around the enormous
house were covered in bright green grass with islands
of flowers artistically scattered about. Thick clusters of
evergreens were positioned to show off the view of the
mountains in the distance.

Penny was fairly certain there wasn't a single piece
of property in all of Wyoming that was so magnificently
positioned and landscaped. The house was certainly the
fanciest one that she had ever been inside. All fifteen
thousand feet of it. And not a single stick of furniture
inside was made of cowhide, sported rough-cut edges or
possessed any hint of rusticness like one would expect
in a small ranching community like Weaver.

"Did you know he would be coming here?"

Penny shook her head. Quinn had only shown up at
Vivian's a couple of times before the Vegas trip, and then
always seemingly in passing. "Didn't you?"

"Well, obviously not." Vivian's voice was dry. She
pushed off the settee and went to the windows, sliding
one large panel open. "Call him."

Penny looked at her boss. "I beg your pardon?"

Vivian gestured toward the window. "Lean out. Call
him. You're young and beautiful. You can get away with
a little undignified behavior like that. He can come in
and have tea with us."

Penny's face flushed. She was going to be thirty in
a few weeks. Not so young. As for beautiful—the only
thing she had going for her were her eyes. Supposedly,
she'd inherited them from her father. She'd never known

him. It was just the story her mother always told Penny whenever she'd sobered up enough to get her back in custody for a while.

Until the next bender—then back into foster care Penny went.

Quinn called you beautiful, too.

"Well?"

Vivian was waiting, her hand on the hip of her designer suit.

Clearly, Penny didn't have a graceful way out. She could have pointed out to Vivian that they never "had tea," but figured it wouldn't be wise. "Who says *I* want to be undignified?" Though she rarely worried about whether she was dignified or not.

That was purely a Vivian thing.

"If you don't call him, I'm going to be more certain than ever that something occurred between the two of you this weekend." Vivian's voice was light. But there was a canny look in her eye that worried Penny.

There wasn't a window screen—Vivian felt they obscured the view and belonged *only* in their proper place—the downstairs sunroom. So Penny walked over to the open window and leaned her head out. "Quinn!"

"He'll never hear you all the way out there like that," Vivian chided. "Give a good shout."

Penny inwardly sighed. "*Quinn!*"

"That's better, dear." Vivian peered expectantly through the windows, but still Quinn didn't even glance over his shoulder toward the house. "Well." She sat back down on the settee. "You'll just have to go out and get him." She propped her glasses on her nose and turned her attention to the papers she'd been going through all morning. "Go on, now. And tell Montrose on your way that we'll be having tea in the conservatory."

Montrose was Vivian's regular chef. He'd worked for Vivian in Pennsylvania for years and a prissier, snottier prima donna didn't exist as far as Penny was concerned. Typically, she avoided him like the plague.

And he, her.

But Penny knew there was no point in arguing with her boss, so she left the office and headed through the house and down the main staircase—marble, of course— to the kitchen, which was located on the main floor. When she didn't find Montrose fussing in that cavernous room, she knocked on the door to his private quarters located behind the kitchen.

He opened the door immediately and glared down at her. "What do you want?"

She smiled sweetly. The tall, bald-headed man should have learned by now that looking at her as if she were a bag of doggie-doo left on his porch made no impact on her. Not considering the way she'd grown up. Until the Bennetts, she'd been left so many places she'd felt as wanted as that bag of doggie-doo. "Mrs. Templeton would like tea, Mr. Montrose."

He sighed loudly, running his lined hand down the front of the starched white apron he wore over a severe black suit and white shirt. Unlike most days, when he had a black bow tie circling his turkey neck, today he was sporting a gray patterned cravat. "How many times do I need to tell you it is simply *Montrose*. Not mister. Just Montrose. Surely, even *you* can manage it." He had a faint British accent that tended to come and go, which always made Penny wonder if it was an affectation or not.

With Montrose, it was anyone's guess.

And if she couldn't avoid him, at least she could annoy him. "Of course I can remember, Mr. Montrose. She'd like it set up in the sunroom."

His nostrils flared. "You mean the conservatory."

"Same thing, in my book." She raised her eyebrows. "Can she expect tea, then?" She knew he considered her an entirely inappropriate choice as their employer's personal assistant, because he'd told her so when she'd first been hired and about a hundred times since.

"I suppose." He slammed the door in her face.

She probably should have felt guilty over feeling a little more chipper as she walked away.

There was a spacious atrium in the very center of the enormous house from which you could exit either to the front of the house or the rear.

She went out the rear, crossing the herringbone-patterned brick patio that ran the entire width at the back of the house, then stepped onto the thick, green grass as she headed for the trees.

She hadn't gotten halfway there before her Montrose-inspired spurt of cheerfulness faded.

The sun was high in the sky and even though the air didn't carry the sense of being inside a pizza oven the way it had in Las Vegas, it was nevertheless extremely warm. She was wearing a lightweight cotton sundress, but she still felt hot by the time she neared Quinn.

He was sweating, too. She could see the sheen of it on his corded arms beneath the dirt-smeared white T-shirt he wore along with beige cargo shorts.

He had a wheelbarrow full of mulch and as she approached, he moved farther along the thicket of young trees before dumping another pile of woodchips and then crouching down to spread it in a circle beneath the tree. As he worked, the T-shirt stretched tightly across his long back, and her mouth went a little dry.

It annoyed her probably as much as she annoyed Montrose.

"*Quinn*." He still didn't glance at her, and even more irritated, she walked around the wheelbarrow. "*Quinn!*"

He finally glanced up and straightened, tugging the tiny earphones she hadn't noticed before out of his ears before pushing up the bill of his ball cap. "You look pretty today."

It was the very last comment she could have expected. "Uh…thanks." She could feel her neck starting to flush. The only thing she could seem to think about was the wedding ring he'd tried to foist on her the day before. She hadn't wanted it. He hadn't wanted it. For all she knew, he'd tossed it in the trash. A giveaway pile. She focused on the USAF emblem embroidered on the front of his cap. "What are you listening to?"

"Bach."

"Haven't heard of them."

"Johann Sebastian Bach?" A faint smile played around his lips as he pulled the wire from behind his neck and handed the two earbuds to her. "The Brandenburg Concertos."

The heat went from her neck up into her cheeks. She held one of the earpieces close to her ear, and sure enough, she heard the strains of distinctly classical music. She handed him back the earphones. "I would have pegged you as hard rock all the way."

"Listen to that, too." He draped the lightweight contraption around his neck, but didn't put them back into his ears. Instead, he pulled a cell phone from one of the many pockets on his slouchy cargo shorts and hit a few buttons, then tucked it away again. "And most everything in between. This is relaxing stuff, though."

"You're in need of relaxing?" She made a face and looked away. "Can't imagine why."

"Yeah, well, strangely enough, it's not because of our

unintentional wedded bliss. I sent the vial from Vegas to a friend of mine this morning to test it. It'll be a day or two before she gets back to me." He grabbed the wheelbarrow handles and rolled it forward another few yards before dumping another pile.

She chewed the inside of her cheek and followed him. There was probably something wrong with her when she felt more interested in who his *female* friend was than what kind of substance was in the vial. Whatever the results were, the situation wasn't going to change.

And she was *not* jealous of some unknown woman. "Your grandmother sent me out to tell you to come in for tea."

He looked skeptical.

"You think I'd make that up? She wants to have tea with you." She rubbed her earlobe and shifted from one foot to the other. "And she's uh, well, she's—"

"Spit it out, sweetheart."

Her face was hotter than ever. "Suspicious!"

"Why?"

She gestured. At him. At the trees. At the mulch. "What are you even doing here?"

"Relaxing."

She waited a beat. Because even she wasn't buying into the explanation. "You couldn't relax somewhere else? You had to show up here, without your grandmother even expecting you?"

"Of course she's expecting me. I ran into Josh McArthur in Braden. He was picking up the mulch at the nursery. Complaining about having to drive all the way back here. I had to come to Weaver anyway, so I offered to take care of it. He called to let her know. I was standing right there when he did it."

She frowned. "He spoke directly with your grandmother?"

"I thought he did." He looked past her toward the house.

Concern overrode everything else. "Vivian said she wasn't expecting you. She seemed genuinely surprised."

"Which would mean she's starting to forget phone calls that happened within half a day?" He gave her a sharp look. "What else is she forgetting?"

"Nothing that I've noticed!" She hated the defensiveness in her voice. "She's been as sharp as a tack today. Same as every day. It's exhausting just keeping up with her. Are you *sure* Josh spoke with your grandmother? Maybe he left a message with Montrose."

Quinn was already pulling his cell phone out of his pocket again. He dialed a number and held it to his ear, only to swear softly a moment later as he hung up and pocketed the phone once more. "Not enough signal for a call." He put his hand on Penny's elbow and steered her toward the house.

She practically had to jog to keep up with his long-legged stride. By the time they reached the house, she was breathless.

Montrose was just crossing the atrium, holding a well-laden silver tray in his hands. He gave them both a disapproving look, though he stopped short of saying something. Probably only because Quinn *was* Vivian's grandson.

"Montrose," Quinn's tone wasn't quite commanding, though it came close enough to have the older man slowing to a stop. He'd pulled off his cap when they entered and he tapped it against his thigh. "Did you receive a message this morning for my grandmother?"

"I receive many messages for Mrs. Templeton," Montrose informed in his snippy, superior tone.

Quinn's lips curved into a smile that struck Penny as

oddly dangerous. "About me bringing the mulch instead of her landscaper?"

Montrose's nose wrinkled, but he held his ground. "I don't divulge Mrs. Templeton's business to other people."

"Oh, for crying out loud, Montrose," Penny snapped. "Quinn is hardly other people."

Quinn took a step closer. Montrose was tall and skinny, but Quinn dwarfed him. So much so that Penny had a sudden image of Montrose snapped in half like a matchstick. "You're loyal to my grandmother. And I can respect that. All I want to know is if you got a message that I would be here today. Simple question. Simple answer."

"Well, Montrose?"

They all looked up to the second-floor landing that surrounded the atrium on all four sides. Vivian was standing at the fancily patterned wrought iron balustrade, looking down at them.

"Madam?"

Vivian clearly didn't buy his innocent tone. "I can send you back to Pittsburgh, Montrose, just as easily as I brought you to Weaver."

Montrose raised a haughty eyebrow. "Please, do. I much prefer the quality of your guests at Templeton Manor."

Penny controlled her impatience. Such exchanges were typical between her boss and the chef.

"Montrose, Montrose," Vivian tsked as she walked along the landing toward the staircase. "You're being deliberately difficult. You know I'm the only one in this household who is allowed to be difficult. Answer my grandson's question."

Montrose gave a grudging nod to Quinn. "Yes. I received a message."

Penny's relief was so great, she had to sit down on one of the tapestry-covered chairs situated in the center of the atrium. "Why didn't you tell her, then? Did you forget?"

Montrose looked down his nose at her. "I do not forget anything."

Vivian was coming down the stairs. "Set up the tea in the conservatory, Montrose."

He looked like he wanted to fling the silver set onto the marble floor. But he inclined his head before striding off.

"Don't mind Montrose," Vivian told them. "He's been in a snit with me since yesterday when I told him I preferred Mr. Bumble's quiche over his."

Penny could imagine that. Robert Bumble, more commonly known as Bubba, was a short-order cook at one of Weaver's local diners. He was a tatted-up biker-looking brute who, in comparison to Montrose, was as sweet as a baby lamb. And he cooked for Vivian on Montrose's day off.

"Better Montrose's prissy snit than you starting to lose your marbles," Quinn said, dutifully dropping a kiss onto the cheek Vivian presented to him.

Rather than take offense, Vivian chuckled. "Very true, darling. Montrose and I know each other far too well. Soon enough, he'll latch on to some new reason to justify the stick stuck up his derriere."

Penny bit back a choked laugh.

"I just need to wait him out," Vivian concluded. "On another note, Quinn dear. You do know that you're very sweaty. Penny will show you where you can tidy up a bit before tea." As if agreement was a foregone conclusion, she sailed after Montrose.

Neither Penny nor Quinn looked at each other until long after the echo of Vivian's footsteps died.

And even then, Penny quickly looked back at her hands that she'd been rubbing nervously together. She finally stood and led the way out of the atrium, opposite the direction Montrose and Vivian had taken. "You can use one of the guest baths. There are literally a dozen bathrooms in the house. I suppose you knew that, though." She couldn't seem to keep herself from chattering.

"No."

She glanced at him, then away. He was too disturbing for her peace of mind. "Oh. Well. Twelve bathrooms like I said." Could she possibly sound chirpier? It was embarrassing. "Ten bedrooms. Two kitchens if you count the one in the guesthouse on the other side of the garages. There are four, you know. You should know. You've been here before. Didn't you get a tour?" She hauled in a breath.

He shook his head. He looked amused. Probably at her inability to just…shut…up. "Still don't understand why she wants such a huge house like this."

"I hear it's much smaller than what she's used to." Penny pushed open a heavy wooden door and the floor switched from marble to carpet. "And she expected Hayley to live with her." Hayley was Quinn's cousin and had been the only one at first to welcome Vivian's arrival in Wyoming. "But that was before Hayley and Seth got married. Naturally they wanted a place of their own." She was still telling him things he'd naturally know about his own family.

What was *wrong* with her?

She knew what was wrong with her. If she kept talking, then he wouldn't have a chance to. And if he didn't have a chance to talk, then he couldn't bring up the wedding ring. Or the wedding certificate. Or anything else at all.

"Vivian still wouldn't have needed this much space," Quinn said. *Not* about their wedding. Not about anything to do with Penny at all. "Ten bedrooms? What'll she ever use them all for?"

"Well, Montrose has one." The carpeted hallway was very wide, easily allowing him to walk alongside her. She walked a little faster, trying to take a lead. "Then there's a bedroom for the housekeeper if Mrs. Templeton ever finds someone to replace Britta since she quit. We can thank Montrose for that, too. They were constantly fighting. Another bedroom in the guesthouse. I don't know who Vivian is hoping will ever use that—but it feels like she's holding out hope for someone in particular. Someone who'll use it more or less permanently."

"You?"

She laughed nervously, because he had more than matched her pace with his own. "Hardly." Even though the hallway was wide, his arm still brushed against hers.

Was he doing it deliberately?

"Why hardly?"

"Because she's never offered and I've never asked. I rent a bungalow in town that is smaller than the guesthouse. That's far more my style. More likely, she'd be thinking about *you*."

"There isn't anything permanent about my being in Wyoming."

The reminder that he'd be gone soon enough ought to have been a comfort. She wasn't sure, exactly, why it wasn't.

"And the rest of the bedrooms are upstairs," she concluded swiftly. She wasn't going to let herself think about Quinn's staying *or* going. It was a pointless exercise. "Mrs. Templeton's master suite is one of the rooms, of course. Your grandmother expects that when she has guests, the house will be quite full." She stopped next to an open doorway and gestured, a la Vanna White. "Here you go."

The second he passed through the doorway, she turned to go.

But he caught her wrist, stopping her. "Wait."

She pressed her tongue hard against the back of her teeth and resisted the instinct to yank away. "You don't know how to find the conservatory," she surmised.

"It's a house. Pretty sure I could manage to find the conservatory." His fingers tightened and she felt herself being tugged into the spacious bathroom.

Which meant he was going to bring up the ring. The wedding.

"Quinn, this isn't the place to—" he pushed the door closed and let go of her "—talk about it," she finished, unconsciously rubbing her wrist.

So much for spaciousness. With him looming over her, she felt positively hemmed in.

"Vivian isn't bugging the bathrooms for sound, Penny."

She couldn't help backing up until her rear end hit the door behind her. "No, but that doesn't mean we should be here like this."

He gave her a look. "This?" He tossed his hat on the counter and turned on the water taps above the hammered copper sink before plucking one of the sea shell-shaped soaps out of a crystal bowl. He thrust his hands beneath the water and the soap shot out of his grip.

It flew straight at Penny, hit her in the chest and bounced onto the floor, coming to a rest next to her sandal.

It all seemed so ridiculous, she didn't know whether to laugh or cry.

She leaned over to pick up the wet soap, then dropped it in his outstretched palm and wiped her hand down the side of her sundress. "If she sees us spending any time together she's going to think she's on to something where we're concerned."

"And she'd be right. But if she sees us avoiding each other, she'll think the same thing." He lathered up his forearms and awkwardly rinsed them in the sink. The copper bowl was definitely pretty. But it wasn't exactly user-friendly when it came to a man of his size.

"Marvin Morales filed the paperwork."

He bent over and sluiced water over his face, then the back of his neck. He didn't seem to care that he was splashing water on either the copper-framed mirror or his T-shirt.

She, however, had a lightbulb moment of understanding why a wet T-shirt contest held so much appeal to some people. "Who's Marvin Morales?"

He turned off the taps and gave her a strange look. "The guy who married us." He snatched a thick hand towel off the stack of folded towels and swiped it over his face.

"Oh. Right." She couldn't feel more idiotic. "I'm not sure I knew that was his name."

"Doesn't matter." He started drying off his arms. "The point that does matter, though, is that he filed the paperwork. Which means it is official." He tossed the towel down on the gleaming black quartz surface next to his hat. "Like it or not, darlin', you and I really are husband and wife."

The bathroom was suddenly a swirl of black and copper. She could feel her knees start to go. Could feel herself sort of sliding down the door behind her back and felt helpless to stop it.

Quinn leaped forward and stopped her before she landed on the ground. "Hold on there." As if she weighed nothing at all, he lifted her and set her on the counter. "Put your head between your knees."

She couldn't do anything but, considering his hand holding her in place. With his other hand, he turned the water on over the towel he'd just used. Then he squeezed it out and placed it against the back of her neck. "Do you get light-headed a lot?"

She could feel water crawling down her shoulders. "No."

"Never fainted before?"

Once. A long time ago. When she'd answered the door to find an army officer wearing his dress uniform standing there. A chaplain had been with him.

And she'd known. Without either man having to open their mouths, she'd known that Andy was gone.

"Never," she lied. She pushed aside the cold, wet towel and sat up.

"Slowly."

She ignored him and slid off the counter, tugging the knee-length skirt of her sundress down where it belonged. "I'm fine." That was a lie, too. Because she wasn't fine. She felt like the world was turning sideways and that gravity no longer existed. "Your grandmother's waiting."

"And she can wait a little longer. We both don't need to go off half-cocked in our own directions trying to resolve this marriage thing."

"Right." She sidled backward toward the door.

"We need a plan."

"Absolutely." She blindly felt behind her.

"Once we know you're not pregnant."

"I'm not."

"How do you know for certain?"

She opened her mouth. Closed it again.

"That's what I figured," he murmured. "*If* and when we know you're not, then we'll hire an attorney who can handle things. An annulment or...whatever."

She nodded quickly. The doorknob turned in her hand. "Yes."

"I have two cousins who are lawyers. Archer and Rosalind. Either one would—"

"No!" The door she'd been opening accidentally bounced against her backside and slammed shut. "I told you I don't want anyone here knowing about this. That includes your cousins!"

"They're lawyers, Penny. Confidentiality *would* apply, whether we're related or not. I know Arch would be happy to do it. It's his house where I've been crashing."

She shook her head adamantly. "It has to be someone else."

"You're being unreasonable," he said calmly. "You do know that, right?"

"I *want* someone different. Someone who doesn't know me from Adam! If you won't find someone, then I will."

Chapter Six

Quinn couldn't ignore the panic filling Penny's eyes. If there was one thing he was accustomed to dealing with, it was someone in the throes of panic. And God knew focusing on her was better than the way he'd been dwelling on the thorny conversation he'd had that morning when his commanding officer tried to force a promotion on him.

It was always that way.

Save someone else.

No matter what.

Only she wasn't a mission. She wasn't a job.

She was Penny.

His wife.

Something twinged inside him. Something that had nothing to do with his job or his injuries or the regulations that were still keeping him from being placed back on flight status.

Something that had everything to do with *her*.

"Okay," he soothed. "I'll find someone else. Someone who doesn't know either one of us from Adam."

But she seemed beyond listening. "I don't want *any-one* we know learning about this! Not your cousins. Not friends. Particularly not your grandmother. Can you imagine what she'd think of me?"

He lifted his hands peaceably. "Considering she's had quite a few marriages of her own, I doubt Vivian would be as judgmental as you think, but I understand. I'll handle it. When was your last period?"

Penny had fisted the sides of her sunny yellow sundress in her hands, and her vivid eyes that had been clinging to his immediately shied away. "A, uh, a little while ago."

"How little?"

Her lips pressed together.

"Penny?"

She huffed out a sigh filled with frustration. "A couple weeks ago."

No wonder she hadn't wanted to tell him.

They couldn't have timed it better if they'd been planning to conceive.

Which they weren't.

He was too well versed in examining every possible angle of a situation before letting the pucker factor get too high, though. There were worse things than an unexpected chance at fatherhood. Or, he reminded himself, a CO who wanted to push Quinn into a position he didn't want.

They weren't dead. They had all their body parts intact and functioning.

He looked away from the swell of her breasts. *Definitely* functioning.

"Is your cycle pretty regular?"

She flushed and gave a reluctant-looking nod. Her gaze bounced around the bathroom, hitting every corner but where he stood two feet away from her.

"So we should know something in another few weeks?" She didn't answer right away and he shifted slightly until he caught her gaze with his own. "*Penny*?"

She finally nodded again. "Your grandmother will be wondering what's keeping us." She reached behind her to open the door again. This time she successfully navigated the doorway as she hurried out into the hallway.

He let her escape. How could he not, when it was so obvious that she wanted to get away from him?

He waited until she was no longer in sight before he wrung out the wet towel and hung it over the edge of the sink to dry.

Then he took his time wandering back through the house and by the time he made it to the conservatory, Penny was already there and sitting in one of the cushioned iron chairs situated around a low table. A silver tea service was arranged on the glass surface, along with a plate of scones and fancy-looking little desserts.

"So this is a conservatory," he said as he walked into the room. Vivian smiled at him. Penny jumped as if she might have actually hoped he wouldn't have found his way there. "Fancy name for a sunroom, if you ask me."

"Old habits die hard," Vivian said, unperturbed. She gestured at the chair across from Penny. "Make yourself comfortable, dear." She picked up the silver pot and began pouring tea into a china cup.

He wasn't sure the chair was exactly meant for comfort, but he sat where she wanted and tossed his cover on the floor beside his chair. Penny's eyes met his briefly before skittering away. She had a cup and saucer sitting on a tiny glass table beside her chair, but it looked untouched.

"Milk or sugar, dear?"

Given the choice, he was a coffee guy. First, last and always. But he could drink most anything when he had to. "Straight up, thanks."

His grandmother set down the pot and handed him the cup and saucer. "A scone? Montrose's really *are* the best."

"I'm sure they are. But the tea's enough." Feeling like he might break the delicate flowered cup if he wasn't careful, he took a sip. As he'd anticipated, the hot liquid tasted as appealing as dirt. Gulping it down to get rid of it probably wasn't the politest course. He forced another sip and set the cup and saucer on his own tiny chairside table. He glanced around at the potted plants artfully dispersed throughout the large, window-lined room. "Does Montrose take care of the plants in here?"

"He'd have a stroke if I even suggested it," Vivian said drily. "He's a chef. Anything outside chef-ly duties is out of the question. Right now, since I haven't been able to find someone regular, I'm taking care of them myself." She caught his look. "I'm capable."

"Never thought otherwise," he assured. It was his dad and his uncle who were convinced Vivian was a menace to everyone, including herself. Aside from a few eccentricities, as far as Quinn could tell, she was harmless. "The palms look good." Though he considered the exotic, lacy-looking fronds entirely out of place in the middle of Wyoming.

"Thank you. I had this room designed for special lighting when it's needed."

It seemed like a lot of fuss to him to grow plants outside their natural environment, but then it wasn't his money Vivian was spending. And she had more than enough to waste however she wanted.

He leaned forward to snag one of the tiny frosted cakes

and popped it into his mouth. The confection melted on his tongue. If it was an example of Montrose's prowess, it was a good one.

Penny was still sitting there silently, though she'd begun pleating one edge of the white linen cloth spread over her knee.

He wished he could alleviate her tension. But anything he did or said now would be in front of his grandmother, which he knew Penny didn't want.

He swiped another little cake and sat back, propping his ankle on his knee. "So how is the big political campaign going?"

"Oh, simply excellent." Vivian looked at Penny. "Go get your computer, dear, so we can show Quinn what we've been working on."

Looking relieved, Penny hopped to her feet and quickly left the room.

The second she was gone, Vivian's gaze sharpened on Quinn's face. "I want to know what's going on between you and Penny. And—" she lifted her hand before he could open his mouth "—don't tell me 'nothing.' I may be old but I am not blind. And she's becoming a very dear girl to me."

He'd faced down superior officers who didn't have the steely-eyed look she was giving him. If he hadn't promised Penny, he would have just told Vivian the truth.

But he had promised.

And he didn't break promises.

"Maybe not, but you are imaginative," he said.

"Please," she scoffed. "I see the way you look at her. I see the way she looks at you, when she thinks I'm not looking." His grandmother rose and went over to fuss with the potted palm sitting in the corner of the room. "Arthur looked at me like that, when we first met." She picked up a fancy gold spray bottle and spritzed water over the fronds. "Of course I thought he was being very fresh." She sent him a quick smile over her shoulder. "At my age, it was ridiculously flattering." She set down the bottle and wandered closer to the windows. "I do like the view here," she murmured. "You know, I really didn't expect to."

"Like the view?"

"Like anything. *Wyoming*." She drew out the word, shaking her head. "Arthur would have loved it here."

"You miss him a lot."

She glanced at him again. "Don't mistake me. I loved your grandfather with all my heart. But Arthur? He was the love of my life." Her gaze went past him and she smiled. "Ah, Penny, dear. Set up the computer on the table there. Quinn, just finish eating those petit fours. You've already had most of them anyway. Then move the tray, please."

He took the remaining squares and shoved the tasty bits in his mouth. He moved the tray, and Penny set her computer on the glass table.

"Sit there with Penny." Vivian gestured. "You'll see the computer better."

He stifled a sigh and sat next to Penny. She was busily typing on her laptop but she was stiff as a board.

"Show him the campaign poster," Vivian told her. "Without the purple."

Penny's gaze flicked to his for a moment. She'd already pulled up an image of the poster. "No purple," she assured.

Quinn looked at the computer screen, giving what he hoped was a suitably impressed nod at the Templeton for Town Council display. "Is there a print shop in Weaver?"

Vivian looked at Penny. "That's all in Penny's capable

hands." Montrose entered the room and she gave him an annoyed look. "What is it now, Montrose?"

"You have a phone call." He didn't look pleased delivering the message. "Mr. St. James."

Vivian, however, looked very pleased. "Thank you, Montrose. I'll take it in my office." She started to leave the room, following her chef. "Penny, dear, make sure Quinn has more tea."

In her absence, silence descended.

Penny closed the laptop and stood. She picked up the teapot, clearly intending to refill his cup.

"I'd rather suck on the mulch I was spreading outside."

She pressed her lips together, looking almost like she wanted to smile as she set the pot back down on the silver tray.

There was no reason for him to stay there. It didn't make a hell of a lot of sense that he felt reluctant to leave. He stood. "I'd better finish the mulch."

"Your grandmother does employ people to handle the grounds." Her gaze seemed focused on his chest and he realized he'd pressed his hand to the ache in his side.

"I know." He leaned over and grabbed one of the scones from the tray. There was a set of glass doors leading out to the brick patio and he headed toward them. "Tell Vivian I'll be in touch."

Worry filled Penny's eyes and he knew it wasn't on his grandmother's behalf. But he was hanged if he knew how to make things better. He couldn't go back in time to prevent Lansing's damn-fool stunt in Las Vegas. They could only go forward and deal with the situation that they did have.

It was true when it came to Penny.

And it was true when it came to his entire career.

As he pulled open the door and went outside, he wasn't sure which one was going to be more of a problem.

"Thanks, Sherry." Penny nudged the credit card receipt she'd just signed back to the woman behind the counter at the print shop. "I appreciate the quick turn-around on the posters." It had only been two days since Vivian approved the design and instructed Penny to show it off to Quinn.

Sherry was grinning. "I appreciate the business." She patted the plastic-wrapped stack. Templeton for Town Council was visible through the film. "You could have had them printed in Weaver."

"I didn't even consider it," Penny admitted. Sherry had always done the printing for Dr. Templeton when Penny had run his practice. She had experience with Sherry Clemmons's shop, and none with the new Copies-n-Print business in Weaver. She picked up the heavy package of posters. Given the opportunity, Sherry would talk her ear off and Penny still had a few errands to take care of once she drove back to Weaver.

"Are George and Susie still in Florida? My folks are debating retiring in Florida versus California. Mom wants Florida, of course, since that's where my aunt is. So—" Sherry's eyebrows went up "—how are they doing?"

Her former schoolmate wasn't talking about her own family. She was talking about the Bennetts who'd moved to Florida after Andy died. "Fine, last I heard." It was truthful, albeit entirely misleading since Penny had avoided her foster mother's attempts at communicating with her since they'd left Weaver. It was cowardly on Penny's part, but it had always been too painful. At the time, Penny hadn't been able to share her grief over Andy with anyone. Not even the family that Susie and George had become to her.

Uncomfortable with the reminder, she pushed her hip against the door, opening it. "Gotta run, Sherry. Thanks again for the quick turnaround."

"You bet."

Outside, Penny's car was parked at the curb and she balanced one end of the bulky package against the roof so she could open the passenger-side door.

"Need some help there?"

She looked over to see David Templeton coming out of the bank next door. Ordinarily, the sight of her former boss would have brought nothing but pleasure. But she hadn't seen Dr. T since before the Las Vegas trip, and now all she could think about was the fact that he was Quinn's father.

And she hadn't seen or heard from Quinn in two days.

"I'm fine," she said and quickly dumped the posters inside the car before he reached her. "Just busy running errands for your mother."

The pediatrician wasn't as tall or as brawny as his only son, but he'd otherwise passed on his good looks. Only now did Penny really see the strong resemblance, though.

And Quinn would likely pass on the same thing to his son.

Something inside her stomach squiggled around.

"I heard about her running for the town council in Weaver." Dr. Templeton shook his still-dark head. "It would be typically outlandish if I didn't know she'll never follow through."

Penny wasn't sure about that. "She seems pretty serious about it. She even wants to schedule a debate with the other candidate." A suggestion that had earned Penny an earful from Squire Clay when she'd called the rancher to try and arrange it.

"A debate. For a town council seat." David shook his head. "Don't be surprised if she tries to buy the election," he warned.

"Is that even possible?"

"With Vivian's money and Vivian's penchant for getting her own way, anything is possible." He hesitated for a moment.

"Her health has been fine," Penny offered. "She hasn't even had any doctor appointments in the past several months."

His lips pursed slightly. He inclined his head. "Thank you."

He was a good man. A decent man. And she hated seeing the discomfort in his expression. "How's everything at the office? Margaret still working out all right?"

The lines in his forehead eased. "She's not you, but since I had to replace you, she's been a good choice. I wouldn't have known it if not for your recommendation. The only thing I knew about Margaret was that she was Matty's mom."

The praise made her flush. Matty was two years old now and one of Dr. T's patients. "I'm glad it's still working out for everyone."

"Yes, but don't forget. When working for Vivian becomes intolerable—and sooner or later it will—you'll still have a place at my office. Always."

She didn't think that Margaret would appreciate the sentiment, but Penny did. "Thanks. Right now working for your mother has been fine, though. Varied, that's for sure."

"Delia mentioned the Las Vegas trip. Well—" he smiled ruefully "—she told her mother, who told me.

I hope Vivian at least gave you a little time to yourself to enjoy."

She nodded quickly and jangled her car keys. She wanted to stay far, far away from the topic of Las Vegas. "I'd better get going. And I'm sure you've got the usual load of patients this afternoon." She edged toward the curb. "Give everyone my best."

"I will." He waited on the sidewalk until she'd gotten in her car, and lifted his hand in a wave as she drove away.

The encounter had her so rattled, though, that as soon as she turned at the next intersection, she pulled into the first parking lot she passed, just so she could take a few minutes to gather her wits.

Vivian's image looked up at her through the plastic-wrapped posters.

Everywhere Penny turned, Templetons were there to watch. And her head was pounding as a result.

The parking lot belonged to a small strip of retailers—one of which was Braden Drugs—and after locking her car, she headed toward it. With a cola and a pack of acetaminophen bolstering her, maybe the winding 30-mile drive back to Weaver wouldn't feel quite so tedious.

The small store was cool and a little dim, which was nice after the bright sunshine, and she went straight to the rear of the store where the refrigerator case was located. She plucked a can of soda from the display and pressed it to her neck as she turned to look for the pain reliever aisle.

The sight of a familiar helmet-haired woman, though, had her ducking down the nearest aisle. She had no desire to run into Francine Meyers. One of Penny's happiest days as a teenager had been when she'd been removed from Francine's fostering care. She hovered out of sight until she saw the top of Francine's head moving down another aisle.

Encounter averted, she exhaled and turned.

Stork Stick Special!

Penny nearly ran right into the sign that was listing crookedly from the shelf.

She hesitated. Started to reach for the white box with the image of a stork bearing a baby on it.

"Oh, hey!"

She jumped like she'd been bit and blindly grabbed the closest item to the white box. But it wasn't the dreaded Francine who'd turned into the same aisle. It was Delia Templeton.

And Penny was caught red-handed with a box of condoms in her hand.

She felt her cheeks flush guiltily. "Delia. What, uh, what a surprise."

Delia looked down at the *Braden Drugs* apron she was wearing. "I guess."

The lightbulb went on. "I didn't realize you worked here." Delia hadn't mentioned a thing about a job when they'd gone to Las Vegas.

"I just started," Delia said, looking vaguely embarrassed. She was equally as dark-haired as Quinn, but was as petite as he was tall. "How…how are you?"

"Fine." Delia hadn't seemed to notice the small box in her hand, and putting it back on the shelf would only draw attention to it. "You?"

"Fine." Delia hesitated. "I, um, I'm glad to run into you like this, actually. I never told you how sorry I was for not speaking up about what happened in Las Vegas." She adjusted the Stork Stick advertisement, but the sign slid sideways again.

Delia was only a few years younger than Penny, but

Penny felt decades older. "I think we're the ones who owe you something—our thanks. Quinn told me you dumped out the drinks before we could finish them."

Delia lifted her shoulder. "I'm still sorry." She held out her hand. "I can ring those up for you if you want."

Before Penny could make up some excuse, Delia had taken the condoms and the can of soda from her and was already heading to the front of the store.

Feeling resigned, Penny followed. She supposed the condoms were better than a pregnancy kit. She imagined purchasing *that* would have garnered more curiosity on Delia's part.

Unfortunately, when they got to the register, Francine was already standing there. There also was a clerk ringing up a customer so Delia handed back Penny's items. She grinned a little mischievously. "Tell Quinn I said hello."

Francine had glanced behind her. She gave the box of condoms in Penny's hand a look that set Penny's nerves on edge.

She boldly set them on the counter, right under Francine's judgmental nose and raised her eyebrow, daring her to say a word.

Francine sniffed and turned her back on Penny.

That was just fine with her.

Chapter Seven

"Honey, you're not eating. What's bothering you?"

Quinn looked over at his mother. Season Templeton was as blond as Quinn's father was dark. And even though she'd retired from her psychology practice when she'd had Delia, she still had the ability to see inside his head when he least wanted her to.

Or maybe that was just what all mothers were able to do.

Either way, he didn't want to get into what was bothering him. "Still trying to get used to having good grub." To prove it, he sliced off a hunk of the steak she'd grilled to a perfect medium rare and shoved it into his mouth. The steak was smoky and buttery and pretty much perfect.

It went down like a hunk of sawdust.

And judging by his mother's expression, she knew it.

But she merely passed the salad she'd made along with the steak and baked potatoes to Quinn's dad. "David," she prompted wryly when he didn't even notice because he was busy looking at his cell phone.

"Sorry, hon. Was just checking tomorrow's schedule that Margaret sent." He set down the phone and took the bowl. "I saw Penny in town today." He was busy transferring lettuce onto his plate and missed the way Quinn's attention perked.

His mother didn't, though. She raised her eyebrows a little in his direction as she handed his dad the bottle of vinegar and oil. "Really? How is she? You should have invited her for dinner."

"She's fine. And I didn't think of it in time. She seemed in a rush." David shook the salad dressing over his salad and set the bottle down with a thunk. "Mother's doing, I'm sure."

Quinn caught the faint sigh Season gave.

David jabbed his fork into a chunk of tomato as if he was envisioning his mother's throat. "Running for town council," he muttered. "As if she has the slightest chance running against the likes of Squire Clay. The man's been around forever and done more for this region than any other person I can think of." His voice rose. "But no. Vivian Archer Templeton moves to town and thinks she can throw her money around and everyone'll just hop to. Like always." He looked at Season. "Woman's nuttier than your mother's fruitcake."

"Is that a medical diagnosis?" Season's voice was dry as she ignored her husband's brief rant and turned them on Quinn again. "So how has it been working out staying at your cousin Archer's place?"

"Fine. He's never there." He hoped she wouldn't bring up the fact that he could have stayed with them again. But he was too old to have his mom wanting to make his bed every morning. Which was one of the reasons why he was there for dinner as often as he was. He knew it soothed her bruised feelings if she could at least feed him a couple nights a week. It hadn't been a problem for him until he'd returned from Vegas.

Since then, every time he saw his folks, he thought about what he wasn't telling them.

That he'd had a Vegas wedding.

"Meredith mentioned that he'd been spending more and more time lately in Cheyenne." Meredith was Archer's stepmom.

"Think it was Denver this week," Quinn provided. "Got a new case or something." He wasn't particularly interested in reporting his cousin's whereabouts. But if it kept Season occupied enough to stay away from the subject of *him*, he'd talk about every member of the family until the cows came home.

"Probably a new girl, as well," Season said wryly. "Meredith is afraid he's never going to settle down."

"He's got time," Quinn dismissed.

"Your cousin is closer to forty than thirty," Season pointed out. "Time might be something he should be thinking about if he ever wants to have a family."

Quinn's dad chuckled, his good humor evidently restored as long as he wasn't thinking about Vivian. "Sure you're not really talking about *our* son, honey?"

Quinn returned his dad's grin, but it didn't come easily. Quinn was closer to forty than thirty, too. He was married—even if it was only a legality. And the possibility of a child in the making was disturbingly real.

"I'm not going to apologize for wanting grandchildren," Season told David calmly. "Lord knows that Grace is too busy with her residency, and Delia—" She broke off. "Well, let's hope Delia settles down a little before she starts thinking along those lines."

"That's for damn sure," Quinn muttered.

Which was ironic as hell, since *he* was the one who'd gone off the rails in Vegas.

Season pushed a basket of rolls in front of Quinn. "Do you remember when Penny lived across the street with the Bennetts?"

He dutifully took another roll and nodded before shoving another hunk of meat into his unappreciative mouth.

"Such a shame what happened." Season shook her head. "All these years later and I can tell Susie is still hurting. I hear it in the letters she sends. She and George never took in another foster child afterward. It's such a terrible shame, too. Because they were so devoted to it. Now George is running some charity in Florida to save sea turtles or something."

Quinn forced down the steak with a large drink of water. "Hurting over what? After what?" He knew the neighbors had moved away some time ago, but if his mother had ever dropped details about it in her letters to him, he'd forgotten them.

His dad's cell phone chimed. He looked at the display. Before he'd even set it down again, Quinn's mom was standing up from the table and reaching for David's plate. "The hospital?"

David nodded.

"I'll slice up your steak and make it a sandwich." She dropped a kiss on his head. "You can eat it while you drive." She carried the plate into the kitchen.

Quinn saw the way his dad's gaze followed her slender form.

Was that what Vivian had seen when Quinn looked at Penny?

He gulped down half the water in his glass, trying to drown out the thought.

"How'd your exam go?"

He looked at his father. He didn't want to talk about his appointment at the hospital that afternoon. But he wasn't going to hide it, either. "Not great." He was just glad it hadn't been his final exam with the flight surgeon who would ultimately determine his ability to return as a PJ. He still had at least three weeks before that particular deadline.

His dad waited.

"I'm not getting my range of motion back like I should." He lifted his arm, reaching above his head as far as it would go. Which wasn't as far as Quinn needed it to go. He dropped it back down.

"Physical therapy?"

Quinn picked up his roll and started tearing it into pieces. "Been doing it all along." If Quinn was going to get back to the physical shape his job demanded, he was going to have to step up the pace himself—and hard—whether the physical therapist liked it or not. Or else Quinn would never make it back to flight status.

And a PJ who couldn't fly couldn't be a PJ.

"I know what you're thinking," his dad said. "Don't go overdoing it and land yourself in worse shape."

"I know my limitations." He wisely refrained from mentioning the rock-climbing trip he was considering. Proving he could still hang off a mountain by some rope would be a lot more useful to him than the mild physical therapy routines.

"You knew your limitations, son. Before." His dad didn't have to elaborate on what *before* meant. "Have you put any thought into your options? You've got plenty. You can put your paramedic training to work anywhere. Go back to med school if you wanted. You know that, right?"

"I'm not considering options." Quinn's voice was flat.

Just because options had been swimming in his head since he'd woken up in a hospital bed with half his body in bandages didn't mean he'd seriously considered them.

Isn't Penny an option?

He focused harder on his plate of food. He'd lost nearly twenty pounds since being injured. He didn't need to bulk up for bulk's sake, but he needed to regain some of the muscle he'd lost. Even more important, he needed to get his stamina back up. Hauling hundred-pound bags of mulch around Vivian's "tiny" backyard the other day had left him feeling whipped. It wasn't the weight that had gotten him. It was the endurance of hauling them up and down hills and around the acreage.

Which was piddling compared to what he used to be capable of doing.

"We could've lost you in that attack, Quinn." His father stood. "You've put in a career's worth of time. You're an honest-to-God hero. You've earned a Silver Star. When is it going to be enough?"

Quinn looked up at his dad. "When I know I'm no good to my team." It was the easy answer. The answer he'd known ever since he'd made it through the grueling two-year training pipeline and been awarded his maroon beret.

His mother returned and handed David a wrapped sandwich and a travel mug that Quinn knew would be filled with hot coffee. Like Quinn, his dad drank the stuff around the clock, rain or shine. "Thanks, hon." David kissed Season's cheek, gave Quinn another serious look, then strode out the door.

Season turned her attention back to Quinn's plate. "Is there anything else you would like to pretend to be eating?"

He sighed and pushed aside the plate.

He should have known he wouldn't fool her.

She picked up the plate and brushed his hair back from his forehead as if he was still four years old. "Coffee?"

He nodded.

She smiled faintly as she headed out of the dining room once again. "I thought so."

Penny was mowing the lawn.

Quinn wasn't sure why that surprised him as he pulled up at the curb in front of her small house. It was a normal enough chore for a sunny Saturday in August. Half the town's residents were probably doing the very same thing.

If he was a homeowner himself, he'd be right along with them.

But he wasn't a homeowner. He was a pararescueman who still couldn't para, much less rescue.

Penny's long legs and toned arms were shown off by the pair of fraying denim cutoffs and faded flag-patterned tank top she was wearing. Her long, wavy hair was pulled up in a messy ponytail on the top of her head.

She looked sweaty and young and healthy and if he could have just sat there watching her for the pure pleasure of it, he would have.

Instead, he was going to have to go over there and bring up the matter of their marriage. And he was going to have to watch her expression turn distant and dismayed.

She hadn't noticed him sitting there on the motorcycle he'd borrowed from Archer, yet. Quinn was pretty sure he'd be able to tell if she had and was trying to ignore him. Because if there was one thing he knew for certain about Penny Garner, it was that she had zero ability to hide her emotions.

She just steadily continued working the noisy mower

back and forth across the wide front yard that looked out of proportion compared to the small yellow and white house.

Even though he could have sat there enjoying the show for quite a while, he couldn't put off the inevitable. So he killed the engine and got off the bike. He pulled the square envelope he'd brought with him out of the saddle-bag before crossing the yard. He knew the second she spotted him.

She didn't stop pushing the lawn mower. But all of the natural grace in her movements went stiff. Resistance seemed to scream at him from the set of her shoulders.

She wasn't stiff and resistant when she woke up in your arms.

He blocked out the memory. Just because it had been a memory plaguing him all that week, it was nevertheless a useless one.

And a frustrating one, ending in too many cold showers for a man his age.

He cut across her path. Only then did she stop mowing.

She let go of the handle, and the noisy motor instantly went silent. "What're you doing here?"

"Good afternoon to you, too. I know what was in the vial Lansing used."

Her lips parted. "And?"

"Nothing toxic. Nothing leaving lasting harm." If one didn't count Quinn's and Penny's behavior in Vegas. He held out the envelope. "I also got that in the mail today."

Her hands remained at her sides. Suspicion glimmered in her eyes. "What is it?"

There was no way to soften the facts. "A certified copy of our marriage certificate." He hesitated, in case she reacted like she had at his grandmother's house. He didn't particularly want her passing out on her front lawn since things like that tended to attract the very attention he knew she wanted to avoid. "And a DVD of the actual wedding ceremony."

Her translucent eyes fastened on his. "How on earth did you get that?"

"I was finally able to locate Marvin Morales."

"How?"

"Talking to about a hundred wedding chapels over the last few days." It was an exaggeration, but as he'd worked his way through the listings of the chapels nearest the club where they'd started out that infamous night, it hadn't felt like much of one. He'd called at least twenty before he'd finally hit pay dirt. Not only had he obtained a phone number to talk to Morales directly, but the woman at the chapel had been happy to inform him that he and his beautiful bride had neglected to take home their complimentary wedding DVD recording. "The wedding chapel overnighted it."

Her lips twisted. "How kind of them."

"The lady I spoke with seemed to think it was necessary." Penny still hadn't taken the envelope he was offering and he lowered his hand.

"Did you watch it?"

"I thought it was only right if we watched it together." He flipped the stiff envelope between his fingers. "Who knows? Maybe we'll be so obviously incompetent to enter a legal contract that the marriage police'll declare the whole thing void."

He regretted his flippancy the second hope entered her expression. "Can that actually happen?"

"From what I understand, it's a little more complicated than that. So…" They were both looking at the envelope. "You want to watch it? Beat it into pieces with a hammer? What's your pleasure?"

She rubbed her hands down her cutoffs. "I, um, I only have a DVD player on my laptop."

He dragged his attention away from her shapely hips where she'd rubbed her hands. "Do you have the laptop here?"

She brushed her hands down her thighs again. "Yeah. It's inside."

"I didn't think you were mowing the lawn with it," he said wryly.

She rolled her eyes. Then finally turned toward the house. "Fine. Come in, then."

She couldn't have made her reluctance more obvious.

He stifled a sigh and followed her across the lawn and through the front door.

Inside, the house's cheerful yellow and white attitude was continued, only in a vaguely nautical blue and white.

She went through the cozy living area, through the galley-style kitchen and into the dinky dining room filled by a small round table on which her laptop sat, and two chairs situated opposite each other. "Here." She gestured at one of the chairs.

He automatically ducked his head as he went through the doorway toward the table. The house was probably fifty years old, which accounted for the low door headers. He'd learned as a teenager how to keep from conking his head in similar doorways. He pulled out the chair while she turned on her computer. When he scooted the chair closer to hers, though, she gave him a quick look.

"Be easier to watch if we're on the same side." The words were true in more than one sense.

Her lips pressed together but she focused on her computer when he sat down next to her. He set the envelope on the table, and his shoulder brushed against hers.

He felt her faint shifting away.

The envelope crinkled loudly in the silent room as she tipped out the DVD case. On the front of it was a white and silver label, emblazoned with the wedding chapel's information.

"Happily Ever Chapel?"

"So it says."

She made a soft *mmming* sound and opened the case and lifted out the round disc inside. She pushed it into the slot on the side of her laptop, and a moment later the video blossomed on the computer screen, showing the same logo as the DVD label. She turned up the volume, and piano music started playing.

"Minuet in G Major," he murmured.

"More Bach?" Her voice was sarcastic.

"As a matter of fact."

"Still find it relaxing?"

He let it go. Because the musical piece was barely a half minute long before it looped and began again, and because the chapel logo on the screen had morphed into an image of Penny. She was dressed in a dark purple dress and carrying a round bouquet of white flowers as she walked up a short aisle between two rows of empty white pews. She had a goofy smile on her face and eagerness in her steps.

He felt, more than heard, Penny's long exhale as she watched the screen.

Then the camera smoothly panned to Quinn's face. Which held an equally goofy smile as Penny stopped beside him in front of a wizened little man with a thick shock of black hair.

"That hair," Penny murmured. She shifted on her chair and her shoulder brushed against Quinn's again. "I remember that hair. It was so obviously—"

"Dyed," Quinn finished. He remembered the man, too.

On the recording, Marvin Morales had a distinct Spanish accent. "Dearly beloved," he began. "We are gathered here today—" He looked past Penny and Quinn at the empty pews and gave a shrugging smile before continuing. "To join into marriage Quinn David Templeton and Penelope Ann Garner—"

Penny pressed a key and paused the video. "Shouldn't there be a witness?" She wriggled in her seat, looking at him. "If we didn't have a witness, it can't be legal!"

He pulled the folded copy of their official certificate out of the envelope. "We had a witness." He tapped the signature. "Don't know who the hell it is."

She turned the paper around to peer at the signature. "What's that? Susan? Sandra?"

"Pretty sure it's Shawna. Shawna Smith."

She made a face. "Could be a made-up name."

"Who'd bother? This isn't some conspiracy, Penny. It's a wedding certificate. Our wedding certificate. Shawna Smith probably works for the wedding chapel. She's probably witnessed hundreds of weddings." He reached over her and hit Play.

The video rolled on, zooming in on their faces as they said a few traditional vows and panning out again on the entire tableau just often enough to see the way Quinn slid the ring on Penny's finger, and then the way they melted together as they kissed.

And kissed.

And kissed.

Her hands clasping his head. His hands running down her back. The amusement on Morales's face as he cleared his throat and told them that their wedding night didn't need to take place right there in the chapel.

Penny cleared her throat now, looking red. She shut the laptop, effectively ending the playback.

Then she tucked her hands under her legs and stared at the closed computer.

"Remember anything besides Marvin's dyed hair?"

She chewed her lip. Avoided his eyes as she shook her head.

He knew she was lying. Maybe she remembered now. Maybe—like him—seeing the video had dredged loose the memory of nearly the whole thing.

The way Penny had stared up at him with those luminous blue eyes as she'd promised to love and cherish. The way he'd felt choked up when he'd slid the gleaming band on her finger. He'd bought it for Penny right there at Happily Ever. But they hadn't had a ring large enough to fit his finger and she'd made him promise they'd get one the very next day.

Then they'd said their vows, and Marvin Morales told him to kiss his bride, and Quinn had.

It had felt more exhilarating than diving out of a plane.

Hell. Just watching that kiss had made everything inside him stand up and take notice more eagerly than he'd ever wanted to parachute.

She suddenly stood. "I need something to drink." She went into the kitchen and yanked open the refrigerator door hard enough to make the stuff inside rattle. "Lemonade. You want some?"

He felt in need of a drink, too. And one a lot stronger than lemonade. "Yeah. Thanks." He restlessly got up and pushed the chair into the table. He ducked his head as he went into the kitchen, which really was only big enough for one person.

Her elbow bumped his when she set two glasses on the counter and filled them. She nudged one toward him before turning back to the refrigerator to replace the pitcher. Then she wrapped her hand around the glass.

"Cheers." He softly touched the rim of his glass to the rim of hers. "To marriage."

The corners of her lips twitched, but it seemed more bittersweet than amused. "Cheers." She took a sip and went into the living room where she curled her long legs under her as she sank into the corner of the couch. A moment later her tennis shoes fell to the floor and she lowered her head onto her arm.

He looked away from her long neck and collected himself as he wandered around the living room, stopping to glance at the items arranged on the shelf next to a small flat-screen television. She had several paperback novels ranging from Tolstoy to Rowling. Considering how dog-eared they were, he figured they got more attention than the television.

She always had liked to read.

The middle shelf held a few framed photographs. He recognized the Bennetts in one. "How long did you live with George and Susie?"

"Four years." Her voice was muffled. She still had her head buried on her arm, the glass of lemonade in her hand apparently forgotten.

"Who's the soldier?" The light-haired private in the picture didn't look like he was old enough to vote. But then that was the way most people looked when they first enlisted in the military. Even Quinn.

He heard her sigh. "Andy."

He waited.

She finally lifted her head. "My fiancé."

He let that rattle around for a moment. "Past or present tense?"

Her gaze slid to his.

"Past," he surmised. The fact that she still displayed a

picture of the guy was also telling. He set his lemonade on the shelf. "What happened to him?"

She gave him a tight smile. "Since you're my 'husband—'" she air-quoted the word with one hand "—I suppose you might as well know."

He waited.

"Improvised Explosive Device." She drew out the words. "A week before our wedding." She drained her lemonade and set the glass on the painted-white footlocker that was serving as her coffee table. "Instead of marrying him, I buried him."

Chapter Eight

Penny's words seemed to echo around her living room and she wished she could pull them back in.

Particularly considering the way Quinn was looking at her now as if she were some sort of piece of breakable china.

Not because she didn't feel breakable. She'd been feeling that way since she woke up in bed with him.

She just didn't like him knowing it.

It was too intimate. Knowing something like that about someone else.

He rounded the footlocker and slid her glass to one side so there was room for him to sit.

She would rather he sat on the other end of the couch than right there in front of her, where she couldn't avoid his eyes so easily.

"I'm sorry," he said quietly. "I didn't realize."

She lifted her shoulder. Why would he? "You weren't here."

"How long ago?"

There was an ominous stinging behind her eyes. "Eleven years ago."

He smiled gently and took her hand between his. "That explains Andy's wet-behind-the-ears look. He looks like he was a good guy, though. Steady. I can see it in his expression."

She was surprised by his observation. "He *was* a good guy." Not much more than a boy. Like she'd been not much more than a girl. Andy had been so good, he'd made her want to be good, too.

"What were you? Kids right out of high school?"

Considering the obvious youthfulness of Andy's photograph, it was an easy guess on Quinn's part. But it still felt like he was reading her mind and she looked down at their hands.

He had a complicated-looking black watch strapped around his wrist. For such an oversize man, Quinn's wrists were surprisingly narrow. Not delicate in any way. But…sinewy. Sexy.

Manly.

She closed her eyes for a moment, remembering to nod in answer. "He was a year ahead of me," she said huskily. "He enlisted right after he graduated. We were supposed to get married the following summer once I'd graduated. Susie planned the biggest wedding in history. At least that's the way it felt to me."

Now that she'd started, the floodgate had opened a torrent of memories. All those wedding details that Susie had loved had overwhelmed Penny. "The only thing I wanted to do was marry Andy and finally have my own real family. But there'd been dozens of dress fittings with a seamstress who lived in Weaver." She glanced up at him with realization. "Maggie Clay, actually."

"Clay. I suppose that means she's one of the many cousins I have yet to meet?"

She mentally worked her way through his family tree. "Squire Clay is her father-in-law. So a cousin of some sort by marriage? I never had any real cousins of my own. Maybe that's why I never quite grasped the finer aspects of second and third cousins. And the whole once-removed or twice-removed deal?" She shook her head. "It's Greek to me."

He squeezed her hand slightly. "Tell me more about the big wedding."

She should have known he wouldn't be distracted. "You can't possibly be interested."

"I most definitely can be interested," he countered gently.

So gently that her throat tightened up all over again. She wondered if he knew how like his father he really was.

Only Penny had never once looked at Dr. Templeton and felt her mouth actually water like it did when it came to Quinn. And she certainly had never woken up in a sweat from vividly erotic dreams like she'd been having about Quinn.

"You're only interested because of what happened in Las Vegas," she dismissed huskily.

"No." He didn't elaborate.

Which was yet another unnerving detail when it came to Quinn.

Instead, he asked, "Did you at least like the wedding dress once it was done?"

"It was really elaborate. Big full ball gown sort of thing." She knew he couldn't possibly care about the details, but she gave them anyway. Because as reluctant as she was to talk about it, the more she did, the harder

it was to stop the words. And at least when she was re-
gurgitating the past, it kept her from thinking so much
about Quinn's damned *manly* wrists. "Really beautiful
but not, um, not my style at all. Susie was happy, though.
The bridesmaid dresses were similar. Ten of them." It was
only because George Bennett was extraordinarily crafty
raising funds that he and Susie had had the resources to
foot such extravagance.

Quinn's eyebrows went up. "You must have had a lot
of friends."

She felt a wry smile tug at her lips. "Not that many,"
she admitted. "Only two were friends from school." She'd
lost track with both of them when they'd moved away for
college. "The rest were girls who were either living with
the Bennetts the same as I was, or *had* lived with them
at one point. All fosters who'd come through Susie Bennett's loving home at one time or another.

"And Andy's side?"

"Oh, he laughed about that. It was easy for him. He
had a lot more friends from school than I did. Plus several guys that he'd met when he enlisted." Her thoughts
drifted again. Her and Quinn's Vegas wedding had been
simple in the extreme…

She blinked. Cleared her throat. "It took Andy an hour
to come up with ten groomsmen. It took me two months
to match them with ladies." She'd been so aggravated.
She'd tried to talk Susie into scaling back the whole deal,
but her foster mom had just laughed the way Andy had.
It was the first wedding she'd ever gotten to plan for one
of her "kids," much less two of them, and she'd intended
to go all out.

Quinn's warm, callused thumb rubbed over the back
of her hand in what she felt certain was meant to be a
comforting way.

But it was just…distracting. Making her feel shivers that she shouldn't be feeling. Particularly when she was talking about Andy.

It was disrespectful. Disconcerting. And entirely disturbing.

So why don't you pull your hand away?

"How'd you and Andy meet?"

She realized she hadn't told him. She looked away from their hands. "He lived with the Bennetts."

He whistled silently, looking as if something had just clicked into place. "Cozy."

"Not like you think. Just about the only times Andy and I ever had a chance to be alone was when we were walking to and from school. And half of those times, we had to walk some of the younger kids to their schools first. We had really strict rules." She felt her cheeks warming. Not that Quinn would have known it by the way she'd behaved with *him*.

He smiled faintly and she wondered if he were reading her mind again. But all he asked was, "How many foster kids lived there?"

Relieved, she counted in her head. "At one time? Usually eight. But there were thirteen at one point." And every single one had been as grateful as Penny had been to be there.

"I don't remember the house being that crowded."

"It wasn't at first. I was fifteen when George found the money to build on two more bedrooms so they could qualify for more kids."

"I remember you at fifteen. I don't remember the construction, though."

So much for thinking he wouldn't make at least *some* reference to her misguided attempt at seducing him. She tried not to think about the heat rising in her neck. "It was after you left town again." She moistened her lips. "Anyway, Andy got placed with them when I was sixteen." She remembered the day like it was yesterday. "On my birthday, in fact."

"Happy birthday, Penny," he murmured.

"Yeah." Her eyes started burning again. Between the way her hormones had annoyingly come out of the deep freeze whenever Quinn was around and this particular trip down memory lane, she felt like a basket case. "I knew when I met Andy that he was different than anyone else. We just...fit." She looked down at her hand again, tucked between Quinn's.

That fits, too.

She restlessly pulled her tingling hand free and pushed off the couch. Her knee knocked into her purse that was sitting on the side table and she grabbed it, quickly zipping it shut to hide the box of condoms that she'd shoved inside it after the drug store episode.

"It's all water under the bridge now." She moved the purse to the shelf where she usually left it, which was near the old photograph of George and Susie. She looked away.

Quinn swung his legs around so that he was still facing her. His hands were casually linked between his spread thighs. Along with the sand-colored T-shirt, he was wearing a pair of beat-up jeans that looked in danger of falling apart from the stress of his muscular thighs. "Is it?"

"What else can it be?" She spread her hands, dragging her eyes away from the fraying denim over his knee. Would a proper wife think about mending them? Or just tearing them off? Annoyed with herself, she made a face. "I was supposed to marry an army soldier. Turns out I married an air force one instead. Suppose that means I have a type?" she asked flippantly.

He didn't comment. Just kept watching her with those dark eyes that were too compassionate for comfort. She didn't want his compassion or his sympathy. She just wanted things back to normal.

She needed things to get back to normal.

Which meant getting their Vegas vows undone as quickly as possible. Because she had no intention of trying to be any sort of wife to a military man.

"While you were playing investigator, did you happen to find a lawyer?"

He nodded once. "Yes. Did you get your period yet?"

"No." She pushed her hands in her back pockets and it dawned on her that her cutoffs weren't in much better shape than his jeans. Inside her pocket, her fingertip was tangled in threads. "I'm not late, though," she added quickly. "So we might as well get the paperwork rolling on our annulment. Divorce. Whatever."

He raised an eyebrow, and a tingle ran down her spine.

"Waiting until we know there's no baby isn't going to hurt."

Her chest felt hot. "I don't know how many times I have to tell you there's no baby."

"Until we know there isn't one." His voice was calm. Infuriatingly so.

"And what if there is?" She didn't believe for one second that she could be pregnant. She'd just *know*, wouldn't she? She'd have to know, wouldn't she? "It wouldn't change anything."

The compassion in his eyes hardened into something else entirely. "A baby would change everything."

She crossed her arms and lifted her chin. "Yeah. For me. Your life would just keep trucking along. You'd ship out the second you could and I'd be here with a baby. We don't need to be married for that. Believe me."

His brows pulled together as he slowly stood.

A nervous frisson skittered up her spine. She barely caught herself from taking a step back.

"I told you before that you were my responsibility now. The same thing goes for the baby."

"Oh my God." She threw her arms out to her sides. "There *is* no baby!"

"*If* there's a baby, the same thing goes." His voice was inflexible. "I don't walk away from—"

"Your mistakes?"

His lips compressed. "My duty."

He couldn't have chosen a word less likely to comfort her. "Andy always talked about duty, too. Right up until duty got him killed. And you're no better. You think I want to hitch my wagon to that again? Not to mention the fact that I'm not in love with you." The very idea sent her head into a tailspin. "Not even close!"

He ducked his head close to hers. "Love's not the issue. Your wagon's already hitched to mine, sweetheart. We're married. Remember?"

Her pulse was pounding in her ears. For a second there, she'd thought he was going to kiss her. And she couldn't tell if she was relieved or frustrated that he hadn't. "As if I can forget!"

"What's all this shouting about?"

Penny jumped nearly a foot at the voice on the other side of her screen door. She pressed her hand to her chest at the sight of her boss through the screen. "Mrs. Templeton. What brings you here?" Why now? When Quinn was there?

Vivian pulled open the door. "I knocked. But you obviously didn't hear. You don't mind, do you?" She stepped inside, obviously not caring in the least if Penny did mind. "Quinn, dear. What a surprise." Her tone said it wasn't a surprise at all.

In fact, her tone sounded wholly satisfied.

Penny sidled out from between Quinn and the bookcase behind her. Vivian had never before sought her out at her home. "Did you drive here?"

"Well, I hardly walked," Vivian said drily. "Of course I drove." She walked into the room, looking around her with unveiled curiosity. "I wouldn't have pegged you for such whimsical decor."

Navy blue and white was whimsical? Penny supposed maybe it was, when compared to the gilt and glamour of Vivian's home. And she'd rather it be thought of as whimsical than boring. "Mrs. Templeton, what can I do for you? Did I forget we had something scheduled?"

Vivian looked at Quinn. "As if Penny ever forgets anything on our schedule," she answered. "The girl's an organizational demon. No doubt she had to learn that working for your idiot father."

She set her old-fashioned pocketbook on the footlocker that Penny's mother had claimed belonged to Penny's father before he'd abandoned them both, and perched on the edge of the couch. "Penny, you wouldn't happen to have something cool to drink, would you? The afternoon is turning out warmer than I expected."

"Of course." Penny warily walked past Quinn into the kitchen. She poured a third glass of lemonade, thinking somewhat hysterically that if another person dropped by unexpectedly, she'd be out of glassware altogether and it would be red plastic cups from there on out. She grabbed a paper napkin and carried it back out to the living room.

Neither Quinn nor his grandmother had moved a muscle. Penny swallowed nervously and set the glass on top of the napkin on the footlocker. "It's just instant lemonade," she cautioned. Her wealthy boss had probably never even tasted such a thing.

"It's delicious." Vivian didn't reach for the glass. Her bright eyes bounced back and forth between Quinn and Penny. "Did I interrupt something?"

"Vivian," Quinn's low voice held a warning that even a stump of wood could have understood.

Vivian smiled. She took her sweet time before reaching for her purse. Before Penny's hope that Vivian meant to leave could fully form, her boss merely opened up the purse and pulled out a folded sheaf of papers. She extended them to Penny. "I've been working on debate questions. Those are my notes."

Penny took the papers. "This is great, Mrs. Templeton, but you know I still haven't been able to get Squire Clay to agree to a debate." She'd told the woman about it the day before, after her third failed attempt to get one scheduled.

"He will. Keep bugging him. It's only a matter of time before he succumbs." Vivian looked confident. "If for no other reason than to tell the world what a horrible person I am."

"I'm sure he wouldn't do that," Penny demurred.

"I'm not."

"Why?"

Vivian looked toward Quinn at his question. "Surely someone in your family has filled you in on my many transgressions, mistakenly believed or otherwise." She snapped her purse shut and folded her hands over it on her lap. Her ankles were crossed neatly. Not a hair of her stylishly short, silvery hair was out of place. "When it comes to Squire Clay, though, they're true enough." Her voice was crisp. Matter-of-fact. "When I was a young woman, I was a judgmental, silly fool. I didn't want Sawyer, your grandfather—" she nodded toward Quinn "—being embarrassed by the existence of an illegitimate sister who happened to be Squire Clay's wife. Back in those days, these things mattered. At least I believed they did. Squire's never gotten over the fact that I didn't welcome Sarah into the Templeton family with open arms. That I did my best to keep Sawyer from openly acknowledging his sister. Then she died and it was too late anyway. Sawyer didn't forgive me, either. But times changed and so did I."

"So you're running against Squire so that you can do what? Make up for insulting his wife by beating him in a town council race?"

"Don't be dim, Quinn. I'm running against him because he's an ornery old fool who wouldn't know progress if it bit him on the nose."

That wasn't exactly the reputation Penny knew about the old rancher, but she intended to keep her mouth shut on that score. "I'll try again to get the debate scheduled," she promised.

"Aim for first Tuesday after Labor Day. That will give us a week before election day," Vivian said. "We need to allow enough time for word to spread in town after I trounce him."

That was one thing Penny did know about, though. "News spreads in Weaver just as effectively as it does in Braden. If you—*when* you trounce Mr. Clay, word will get around just fine to anyone who didn't see it for themselves. It certainly won't take a week." More like a day. Or less.

"That's my hope." Vivian clasped her pocketbook and rose. She tugged down the hem of her lightweight salmon-colored jacket and marched to the door.

Quinn got there before she did and opened it for her. "Thank you for the lemonade, dear," she told Penny. "I'll see you on Monday morning. And Quinn," she said as she stepped outside onto the porch step, "if you want to make an impression on Penny, try flowers. I would even lend you a proper car if you wanted to take her out for a proper date." She gestured at the Rolls Royce parked incongruously in front of the small house. "Maybe even put on your uniform. Seems the least you can do when you've already married the girl."

Silence descended.

Mortified, Penny could only stare.

Quinn was equally silent.

Vivian, no doubt, was enjoying the reaction she'd gotten. "I assume this happened in Las Vegas." It wasn't a question.

Quinn glanced at Penny over his shoulder. "Does anyone else know?"

"Not from me," Vivian assured. "I had my suspicions but until now didn't know for certain." She peered around Quinn's wide shoulders. "Close your mouth, Penny, dear. You look like a gaping fish. I'll see you Monday."

Then she patted Quinn's cheek as if he were a good little boy and turned to walk out to her car.

A few minutes later the engine gunned and the Rolls narrowly avoided colliding with the motorcycle before it purred down the street.

"I didn't tell her," Quinn said when the sound of the engine had finally died away.

Penny knew that. She just shook her head and threw herself down on the couch. She dropped the sheets of Vivian's debate questions on the cushion beside her.

Quinn moved them to the footlocker when he sat down on the cushion beside her. "That was unexpected."

Penny made a soundless snort. "She must have over-heard more than I thought."

"I told you that she wouldn't be as shocked as you feared."

"She might not have been shocked, but I'm not ready to place bets on what she really thinks, either." Penny covered her eyes with a bent arm. The old lady was too unpredictable. She had an obvious tendency to say what-ever she wanted whenever she wanted, if only so she could sit back and enjoy the shock waves she caused.

"It doesn't matter what she thinks."

"Easy for you. You're her grandson. I'm just the hired help."

"She's not going to fire you," he dismissed.

"I think we both can agree that nobody knows what your grandmother will do until she actually does it." She lowered her arm. Stared blindly at her "whimsical" decor.

Images from the wedding video swam inside her head and she chewed the inside of her cheek, trying to think about something else.

But it was futile. Not while Quinn was sitting beside her, his warm arm brushing against hers.

She jackknifed off the couch. "I have to finish mow-ing the lawn." Not waiting for a response or reaction, she stomped outside and across the lawn to where she'd left the lawn mower. She squeezed the handle and leaned over to grab the pull cord. She gave it an unnecessarily fierce yank and the gas engine growled to life. She lined up the mower with her last swath through grass.

Quinn stopped her before she could start forward, though. He was holding her tennis shoes.

She looked down at her bare feet and flushed.

She put out one hand for her shoes, but Quinn ignored

it. Instead, he dropped down on his knee, holding out one shoe for her.

"Come on," he said above the noise of the mower. "Stick your foot in."

Feeling like an idiot, she tucked her foot into the shoe. He tied it and gave her a pointed look. "Now the other."

She glanced around. Mrs. Wachowski, the elderly woman who lived in the triplex across from Penny's house, was fussing with the petunias growing in front of her unit and looking over her shoulder at them every ninety seconds. Dori Wells, whom Penny had quickly learned was one of the biggest gossips in town, was standing in her driveway a couple houses down, either flirting with Howard Grimes or arguing with him. It was hard to tell which. But her bright red-haired head was practically revolving as she kept sending Penny and Quinn furtive glances.

Since Penny had first understood that her family situation was ripe cause for talk, she'd hated feeling the subject of gossip.

And now, Quinn and his Prince Charming act over her tennis shoes was sure to cause exactly that.

"Just let me do it," she muttered, letting go of the mower handle again, which caused the engine to die. She reached down to grab the shoe out of his hand, but he held on to it. "Quinn. Come on." She peered over his head. Dori's curly head whipped around to face Howard again. "People are noticing."

"Yeah, because you're making a big deal out of this."

She huffed and crouched down to his level, only to realize his eyes were full of amusement. "Give me my damn shoe, Quinn."

The corner of his lips kicked up. "Ah. So that girl's

still inside you, after all. Thought maybe you'd forgotten how to swear altogether."

Heat ran under her skin. Rejected by him at fifteen, she'd tossed every foul word she'd ever known at his head. Given her erstwhile mother's example to learn from, the list had been long. "I learned how to choose better vocabulary," she said through her teeth. She held out her hand, palm up. "And I refuse to play tug of war over my own tennis shoe."

His lips twitched. "I'll give it to you for a price."

She rolled her eyes. "Save me." They were still crouched like fools next to the lawn mower. "How much?"

"Only one."

"One what?"

"Kiss."

She glared. "Now I know you're just messing with me."

"Why? Because seeing that video of us kissing to seal the deal got me curious? Aren't you curious?"

She pushed to her feet and crossed her arms. The toes of her bare foot curled into the thick grass. She wasn't going to admit to any such thing whether it was true or not.

And it hadn't taken a video to get *you curious, either.*

She ignored the taunting voice inside her head.

Quinn straightened, too. Standing as close to her as he was, she felt dwarfed by his height. She unclenched her arms and grabbed the mower handle just to steady herself.

He dangled her shoe by the laces. "Well?"

"No, I am not curious."

"You're a bad liar, Penny." He lightly touched her collarbone where she could feel her flush rising up her throat. "This blush gives you away every time."

"That's not a blush," she lied. "That's annoyance."

His smile widened. He trailed his finger up the center of her neck, beneath her jaw and to her chin, which he nudged upward. "You're curious. Just like I am. Curious whether it was just the situation, or whether it was something more."

She pressed her lips together. She wanted to deny it. But he'd know that for the lie it was, too.

"Okay, then." His head slowly lowered toward hers.

Her heart rate went a little crazy. Every cell in her body felt poised for something momentous. She swallowed. Barely managed to stop herself from moistening her lips.

"Here you go," he whispered.

She felt something against her midriff and realized he was pushing the tennis shoe into her hand.

Then he straightened. Gave her a quick, knowing wink.

She suddenly felt like throwing the shoe at his handsome head.

"I'll be out of town for a while," he said as he walked away toward the motorcycle at the curb. "I'll see you when I get back. Try not to get into too much trouble while I'm gone."

She launched the shoe at him. It landed yards short.

His smile flashed as he threw his leg over the big bike.

And then with a roar, he drove away.

Chapter Nine

The following Monday, Penny had to force herself to go to work.

It had been two days since Vivian let on that she knew about their Vegas wedding. Penny hadn't seen or talked to Vivian since then. And who knew what sort of mood she'd be walking into now.

The first person she saw as she let herself in one of the side doors was Montrose.

He was carrying Vivian's preferred silver coffee service and he gave Penny his usual sneer. Neither better nor worse than usual.

In Penny's estimation, Vivian tended to tell Montrose most everything. But maybe she hadn't shared this particular news. That surely would have merited a deeper level of sneerage.

"Good morning, Montrose," she greeted. "Nice to see you looking so cheerful on a Monday morning. How is Mrs. Templeton today?"

"Ask her yourself. She's in the conservatory." He stomped past her and disappeared through the doorway leading to the kitchen.

"Always a pleasure," she murmured after his ramrod-straight back.

She went upstairs to Vivian's office and left her purse there before going back downstairs to the sunroom. She took her laptop with her. Vivian was talking on the phone and pacing the room as far as the long corded phone would allow when Penny got there. Her boss waved her in, pointing to the plate of breakfast muffins sitting on a side table.

The food didn't appeal to her. Maybe because Quinn's ball cap with the USAF embroidered on the front was also sitting on the table. She felt an alarming jolt at the sight of it, wondering if he was there, until she remembered that he'd left it behind the previous week when he'd delivered the mulch.

She filled a glass of water from the crystal pitcher—no plastic water bottles where Vivian was concerned—and flipped open Vivian's leather-bound calendar. Her boss had neatly penciled in several items and since Vivian was still involved with her phone conversation, Penny booted up the laptop and added the notes to the calendar that she kept there, which would also sync with Penny's cell phone calendar.

Vivian had made no secret of her dislike for cell phones. She tolerated Penny's, but she refused to use one herself. She wouldn't even use a cordless phone for the two landlines that ran to the house. Called them all security hazards.

And Vivian considered her town council opponent to be stuck in *his* ways.

Penny was almost done when Vivian finished her call.

Her nerves tightened when Vivian sat down in the chair opposite her and crossed her ankles. "How was your weekend, dear?"

Penny hesitated. She gave her boss a wary look. It wasn't possible that Vivian would have forgotten. Except that she *did* have a brain tumor. She studied Vivian's face a little more closely. But the woman's face was as composed as ever. Perfectly, subtly made up in a manner complementing her age. "It was…all right," she said cautiously. "And yours?"

"Stewart thinks he may have found a buyer for Templeton Manor." Vivian waved languidly at the phone she'd left sitting across the room. "That was him just now. He wants me to come to Pittsburgh to meet them."

Penny closed her laptop. The longer Vivian went without some comment about Penny and Quinn, the more concerned she felt. "Is that usual? I didn't think home buyers generally met the home sellers."

Vivian's lips curved humorously. "Perhaps smaller homes," she said. "Estates like Templeton Manor are a bit different."

Penny would have to take her boss's word for that. One day she hoped to be able to buy her own house. For now, though, she had to be content with renting. "Would you like me to arrange your flight?"

"Our flight, dear," Vivian corrected. "As my assistant, naturally I'd like you to accompany me."

"To Pittsburgh?"

"No, dear." Vivian looked amused. "To Neptune." Her smile turned sly. "That is, of course, if your husband can bear to spare you so soon after the nuptials."

Penny's shoulders sank.

Vivian's eyebrows lifted. "Did you think I wouldn't mention it?"

"No," Penny assured. "I was getting a little concerned that you hadn't."

Vivian made an impatient sound. "I wish everyone would stop worrying that I'm on the verge of losing my wits. The rude thing squatting in my head hasn't changed even a fraction of a millimeter in the past two years."

Penny spread her hands peaceably. "I'm sorry. No more worrying."

Vivian's lips compressed. But her expression was wry. "I appreciate the sentiment, at least. Now. I'd like to leave in the morning. Is that a problem?"

"Of course not."

"Perhaps you should check with your husband before deciding."

Penny shifted, feeling hot and awkward. "Please don't call him that, Mrs. Templeton."

"Why not? It's what Quinn is, is he not?"

"Technically, I suppose, but—" She broke off, hearing Montrose's approach. She knew it was him even before he entered the sunroom, because his footsteps were deliberately loud and excessively measured. He filled Vivian's coffee cup from the silver pot he'd been carrying earlier. Then he gave Penny a bored look and set the pot down with a loud clank.

No courteous coffee pour for the likes of her.

She smiled sweetly at him. "Thanks, Mr. Montrose."

His lip curled downward and he left the room once more.

"He truly detests you," Vivian said brightly.

"And I him," Penny assured.

"All in all, a good day in the Templeton household." Vivian's eyes sparkled. She seemed at her very happiest when Montrose was wallowing in his beloved snarkiness.

It was weird.

But Penny could see that the balance worked equally well for both Montrose and Vivian.

"Back to your trip tomorrow," she prompted.

"*Our* trip," Vivian corrected. "Assuming Quinn won't mind, of course."

"Whether he minds or not is irrelevant. And unnecessary, since he told me he's going to be away for a while."

"Away where?"

"He didn't say."

Vivian's brown eyes narrowed. "Didn't you ask?"

"No." She conveniently chose to overlook the fact that she'd wanted to. Not that Quinn had given her an opportunity to, anyway. She shifted again. "Mrs. Templeton, you don't need to worry."

"That's good, dear. Worry causes wrinkles and I already have more than my share. If I get any more, I'm afraid my dear Arthur won't recognize me when I finally join him. But what exactly do I need not worry about?"

Penny mentally shook her head a little. She still wasn't entirely used to Vivian's references to her deceased husband. "A, uh, about me. And your grandson. You see, it was all just an unfortunate mistake. We're going to untangle the legalities just as quickly as we can."

"That seems a shame when you're so well suited to one another. You would make beautiful children together, no doubt."

Penny couldn't stem the sound of disbelief that rose in her throat.

Vivian picked up her delicate coffee cup and peered at her over the edge. "What's that, dear?"

Penny shook her head. "Nothing, Mrs. Templeton." She grabbed her water glass and took a swig.

"I believe I prefer Grandmother over Mrs. Templeton."

Penny choked on a swallow. Water spilled down the

glass and onto her blue sundress. Before starting to work with Vivian, she'd bought a month's worth of dresses, since Dr. Templeton had warned her that his mother preferred her female employees dress like females. Which, in Vivian-speak, meant dresses. Or skirts. Or anything besides pants.

Vivian plucked a linen napkin from the arrangement of them next to the coffeepot and leaned forward to hand it to Penny. "A truly heartwarming response," she said drily.

Penny flushed. She wiped her wet hand and the wet glass and set it on the little table beside her chair. "I swallowed wrong."

"So I witnessed." Vivian looked unusually relaxed as she leaned back in her chair. She picked up Quinn's cap and turned it in her hands. Studying the front of it. Studying the back of it where Penny saw the letters "PJ" imprinted. Then Vivian studied Penny from below her half-mast eyelids. "Do you have any grandparents, dear?"

Talk about a left turn. Vivian had never shown any interest like this before. "No. I never knew them. I also never knew my father."

"And your mother, poor dear, was worse than useless. Do you have any contact with her?"

Penny shook her head. Her mother had disappeared for good the year Penny had been placed with the Bennetts. Neither the state nor anyone else had made a very concerted effort to find her.

"She had a problem with alcohol, didn't she?"

Penny hesitated. "Did Dr. Templeton tell you that?" It seemed unlikely.

Vivian made a dismissive gesture. "David doesn't tell me anything. He and Carter are equally annoying that way. No, I simply had you investigated."

Penny felt herself pale. "I beg your pardon?"

"Don't look so distraught, darling. Tom Hook did the work for me last year before I hired you. In my position, I can't afford to hire people simply for the sheer pleasure of spiking one of my son's guns." She smiled. "Tempting though that is. And despite the cowboy boots Mr. Hook wears that I find entirely inappropriate for an attorney, he is reliably discreet."

"Great," Penny said weakly. "Why are you just telling me this now?"

"Because it's relevant now," Vivian said as if it ought to be obvious. "So I know enough about your unfortunate mother. And that poor boy you were supposed to marry. You were very young."

Could this morning get any worse? "Eighteen."

"I was only nineteen when I married Quinn's grandfather," Vivian said. "But I knew I wanted to spend my entire life with him." Her smile turned bittersweet. "The unshakeable certainty of youthful love. After he gave me three sons, though, he left me just like your young man left you. Death is death."

"Mrs. Templeton—"

"If you can't manage *Grandmother*, then at least try Vivian."

"Vivian," Penny complied. "I don't know what impression you've gotten, but Quinn and I fully intend to rectify the situation. And we, uh, well mainly *I* prefer to keep it from becoming common knowledge. I'd hoped that no one would need to know."

"I know he appears quite hale and hearty now, but Quinn was very seriously injured, you know." Vivian set the ball cap on the coffee table in front of them.

Penny opened her mouth to respond. Only she didn't

know what to say. She nodded. Her gaze kept drifting
to the hat.

"I know what it's like to lose a son. I don't want David
or Carter to have to ever know what that feels like."

Penny's wits scattered. "I'm sorry. I didn't know."

"Thatcher was my eldest." Vivian sighed faintly. "But
he is a story for another day. My point is that Quinn needs
a reason to stay home. *You* could be that reason."

Penny shook her head. "Mrs. Templeton, trust me. I
could never be that reason. Nor do I want to be." She'd
vowed never to fall for another military man. Because
in her heart, she knew that she would always be their
second choice. Andy had enlisted even though he'd had
plenty of other options to pursue. His grades had been
high enough to get him into most any college he wanted
on scholarship. And even though Penny had pleaded with
him to choose something else, he'd told her he'd be back
for her. Everything would be fine. They'd spend their life
together just like they'd planned.

And Quinn—

She broke off the thought. She wasn't falling for
Quinn. So thinking of him in that context was pointless.

"I've never been reason enough for someone to want
to stay with me," she said. The father who hadn't wanted
her. The mother who'd chosen booze over her. The foster families who sent her "back" because they thought
she was too unruly. The fiancé who'd never come back
to her. "It's just the way it is. I've always known it and
it's not going to change." Her life had become a lot sim-
pler when she'd finally accepted that fact. As far as she
was concerned, longing for things a person was never
going to have was a quick trip to unhappiness. That kind
of unhappiness had ruled her mother. And Penny never
wanted to be anything like her mother.

Vivian's head angled as she studied Penny's face. "What sort of a life you must have had to make you think such a thing," she said quietly.

Penny wished she'd kept her mouth shut. "I wasn't looking for sympathy, Mrs. Templeton. I'm just realistic. Even if Quinn cared about me that way, which he doesn't," she emphasized, "I would only be some sort of sad consolation prize in comparison to his lost military career."

"Oh, dear girl, you're underestimating yourself."

Penny didn't know how to respond to that. She disagreed. Of course she disagreed. She had a lifetime of proof.

"Well. Rome wasn't built in a day." Vivian leaned forward and picked up her cup and saucer. "Now. About our Pittsburgh trip. I'd like the same pilot and crew that we had for Las Vegas. If they're otherwise committed, tell them I'll pay double. That tends to get schedules rearranged."

Penny was relieved at the change of subject. Suspicious over it, yes. But relieved nonetheless, and she quickly began taking notes. "I'll call the charter service immediately."

The following several days passed in a whirlwind of activity, with Vivian anchored firmly at the center.

By the time Penny and Vivian returned to Wyoming, Penny was exhausted. She wasn't sure what that said about her level of stamina that a woman well into her eighties could run circles around her. But she could say that the three-day visit to Vivian's Pennsylvania estate had been eye-opening.

When Vivian talked about her home in Wyoming

being scaled back from what she'd been used to at Templeton Manor, she hadn't been exaggerating.

Without seeing the palatial estate for herself, Penny would never have fully understood just *how* little an exaggeration.

And though the prospective buyer hadn't quite made up his mind yet to buy the massive estate, after personally meeting twice with him, Vivian felt confident that he would. Penny supposed that it was because of that certainty that her boss had decided to return to Wyoming with a few more mementos from her old home than she'd originally planned.

Namely, two large oil paintings of Quinn's grandfather, Sawyer.

Vivian wanted the paintings to go to her sons. And since neither David nor Carter wanted anything to do with her, she tasked Penny with the job.

Which was why Penny was pushing one of the massive paintings carefully up the walkway outside Dr. Templeton's house on the morning after she and Vivian had returned from Pittsburgh.

She'd already delivered the first painting to Carter's house. Fortunately, Vivian's younger son hadn't been there. Dealing with his wife, Meredith, had been far easier. Meredith had helped Penny haul the massive thing into the house where they'd propped it against the fireplace.

Then they'd both stood back to study it.

"Carter's going to hate this." Meredith coiled a long, dark curl around her finger as she stepped closer to the painting. The ornate gilt frame stood as tall as she did. "He'll hate the fact that his mother gave this to him at all." Then she sent Penny a mischievous smile. "Definitely going to be an interesting day when he comes home to see it."

Penny had met Carter Templeton only a few times. In sharp contrast to Meredith's engaging ways, he struck Penny as stern and usually unsmiling. Personally, she was glad she didn't have to be around to witness his reaction. She was just the delivery-and-run person.

She'd left shortly after that and driven to Dr. Templeton's house.

It was Friday, and as she slowly pushed the tall cardboard box containing the well-wrapped painting toward the door, she could see the cars parked next door at the house her former boss had long ago converted into his pediatric offices.

She was tempted to leave the boxed painting leaning against the front of the house and go over to say hello to everyone. But after she finished delivering the paintings, she was driving back to Weaver to meet Squire Clay.

Hopefully.

The rancher still hadn't agreed to the debate. Penny hadn't gotten the slightest hint that he was softening to the idea, nor —despite Vivian's prediction—that he was growing annoyed enough to say he'd do it.

Penny was giving up on phone calls, though. Which was something Squire's wife had suggested when her husband had been avoiding Penny's most recent attempt to reach him. Gloria Clay had told Penny that a face-to-face meeting might have more effect. Squire's wife had even gone so far as to tell Penny exactly when and where she should broach him.

She'd reached the porch steps and she went around to the end of the painting, going up onto the steps. She pushed back on the cardboard box, angling it onto the edge of the first step so she could pull it up the rest. It was awkward and heavy, and given that this was her second such delivery, she was beginning to feel like she'd have to go home for a shower before she dared to approach Squire Clay.

Finally, though, she had maneuvered the painting up onto the porch. She leaned it against the nearest stone-covered pillar and rang the doorbell. She knew that Season Templeton was home. Penny recognized her car sitting in the driveway.

The door opened a moment later and she had a smile ready for Dr. Templeton's wife.

"Penny!" Season looked delighted. "What a surprise. David told me he saw you last week. Come in." She pushed open the screen door and her eyebrows went up when she saw the big box. "The last time I saw a box like that, David was bringing home a flat-screen television that he insisted was not too big for our family room. Now the behemoth takes up nearly an entire wall. Please tell me it's not another one."

Penny chuckled. She was a little surprised that Meredith hadn't called and warned her sister-in-law what was on its way. "It's not a television. But it's entirely possible you might wish it were once you see what's inside."

"Now you've got me really curious."

"You want to open it here, or shall I bring it inside?"

"Inside." Season reached out to help guide the oversize thing through the front door and into the foyer. As soon as it was, she went to get something sharp to help cut the packaging.

Penny had always thought Dr. Templeton's house was pretty swell. Now, having seen the lavish mansion in which he'd grown up, it seemed extremely modest. And a testament to his determination to eschew anything to do with his mother. Even his rightful inheritance.

His brother clearly felt the same way.

Season returned, holding a box cutter aloft. "Here we go." She put the edge of the blade against the cardboard. "Are you going to tell me, or just let me find out?"

"What do you prefer?"

"For Mom? Surprises, always."

Penny's mouth went dry at the deep voice.

She looked up the wide staircase to see Quinn descending. He was dressed in camouflage pants and a tan T-shirt that molded his broad shoulders. Overlooking the absolute hotness of the man—which was a worry in itself—he looked very soldier-y. And that caused another worrying level of apprehension.

It had been six days since she'd seen him last. A lot of things could change in six days. A lot of things could change in six minutes.

Which was about the length of their wedding video that she'd furtively watched. About a couple dozen times now.

"He's right." Quinn's mother was busily slicing open the cardboard. "I like surprises best."

Penny wasn't so sure that would be the case if Season knew that her son and Penny were married.

She couldn't seem to tear her eyes away from him when he reached the bottom of the stairs and joined them.

"Long time no see," he murmured.

She swallowed. And considering the desert-like nature of her mouth, it was a wonder she could swallow at all.

"Oh, my goodness." Season had finally succeeded in peeling away the protective layer of cardboard and cushion wrap and was staring at the elaborately framed oil painting.

"Looks like Dad."

Fortunately for Penny's peace of mind, Quinn moved

closer to the painting, which allowed her to edge farther away. Where she could maybe breathe in some air that didn't feel all used up. Where she could remind herself that just because Quinn was wearing fatigues, it didn't necessarily follow that he was getting ready to deploy.

"It's your grandfather," Season murmured.

"I'm guessing this is Vivian's doing." Quinn slid a look toward Penny.

Even though he didn't need confirmation, she nodded. She felt chilled and rubbed her hands down her arms. Season was probably running the central air conditioning. "We brought some things back from Templeton Manor."

His attention left the painting of his grandfather and landed on Penny in full. "*We*? You went to Pittsburgh with Vivian? When?"

Goose pimples skidded up and down her arms. "Tuesday. We got back last night."

"You didn't tell me you were going anywhere. How long was this little plan in the works?"

She stiffened. "I wasn't aware that I was supposed to report in to you. Not that I knew where *you* were, anyway." She certainly hadn't expected to see him at his parents' house when he was supposedly staying with his cousin. Knowing there was no likelihood of running into him was the only reason she'd felt comfortable bringing the painting there. "And you know Vivian. She decides these things at the drop of a hat!"

She suddenly realized that Season was staring at them as if they'd both grown tails.

"Quinn? What's going on?"

Penny could see the consternation in Quinn's eyes. The only reason he hadn't told anyone about their Vegas escapade was because she'd made him promise not to.

And the only reason his grandmother knew was because she'd overheard them.

Now they were giving his mother ample fuel for conjecture?

Quinn's eyes held Penny's captive. "Penny was supposed to tell me if Vivian did anything crazy."

He'd lied for her.

To his mother.

And Penny figured there would come a price for that. Sooner or later.

Her goose pimples multiplied.

"You know I don't like that word, Quinn." Season was still watching them too closely for Penny's comfort. "From the stories your father tells about Vivian, it's a foregone conclusion that she'll do something outrageous. It doesn't mean she's not perfectly sane. Why are you suddenly so interested?"

He still didn't look away from Penny. "She's my grandmother. I want to get to know her before I go back. That's why I went to Vegas. Remember?"

Before I go back.

Penny went from feeling chilled to outright cold and she finally broke free from his mesmerizing gaze. Thanks to Vivian, Penny had learned what the "PJ" meant on Quinn's ball cap. It was the term that pararescuemen still used. They were guys that went straight into danger if it meant saving someone else.

Being intimately familiar with the scars on Quinn's body, she figured there'd been plenty of danger. And he was going back to it.

And it terrified her. There was no other word for it.

And no explanation for it, when it shouldn't matter as much as it did.

She brushed past him toward the door, gesturing at

the painting. "Vivian is selling the estate in Pennsylvania and she wanted Dr. Templeton to have it," she told Season. "She sent a similar one to your brother-in-law." The paintings had matching frames. But the portraits of Sawyer Templeton were from different times in his life. Vivian had told her the one for Carter had depicted his father shortly after Carter's birth. This one, for David, showed him as a much younger man.

In both, it was obvious that Sawyer Templeton had been a handsome man. He'd passed on those genes. David clearly favored him. And Quinn favored *him*.

She felt something inside her jiggle around nervously.

If her cycle held true—like it had done for the past umptysquat years—she should be getting her period that very day. But she was increasingly conscious that she hadn't been experiencing her usual PMS.

She also was increasingly anxious to leave.

"Evidently they were painted by someone pretty well respected in the art world." She pointed to the signature in the corner. "And the frames alone are valuable, too." She gave Season the same quick spiel that she'd given to Meredith. "If you and your husband don't want the painting because it's too large or because it came from Vivian, she only asks that you donate it to the Weaver Hospital Foundation rather than pitching it in the trash altogether. They've already agreed they'll auction it off for the money." Supposedly there was an art expert on the foundation's board of directors who'd said she would oversee it all.

"And if my husband doesn't donate the portrait?"

Meredith hadn't asked that question, though Penny had been prepared. When it came to her estranged sons, Vivian was careful to cross every *T* and dot every *I*. But Penny still felt odd conveying the answer. Even though she was gaining a better sense of just how incredibly wealthy her boss was, it was out of Penny's realm to talk about money in such large terms. "She'll donate a million dollars more than she already has to the foundation every year in which you and Dr. T maintain ownership of the portrait. The same thing goes for his brother."

Season looked resigned. "In other words, she'll give a *lot* of money to an organization important to our entire community so long as they don't get rid of her gifts to them."

Penny felt her gaze wanting to slide toward Quinn and rigidly controlled it. "I believe that's the general idea." She'd heard time and again from Dr. T how manipulative his mother had been. She supposed this was an example of that, though Penny was hard-pressed to see any down side by keeping the portrait. "Honestly, Mrs. Templeton, I don't think Vivian even cares if the portraits get hung facing the wall in a garage. She just wants her sons to have the paintings of their father. That's all."

She sidestepped to the front door and pulled it open. "Would you like me to take away the packaging?"

Season had a thoughtful expression on her face as she shook her head. "We can dump it in the construction Dumpster across the street."

In the years that Penny worked for the doctor, she'd become practiced at ignoring the Bennetts' house, even though it was so close by. She couldn't stop herself from looking there now, though. And there was, indeed, a roll-off sitting to one side of the rambling house. There was also a For Sale sign in the somewhat neglected yard.

"Who's working on it if it's for sale?" She knew the house had gone through a series of owners since the Bennetts.

"From what I understand, the latest owner's doing

some refurbishing to help spur some interest." Season suddenly reached out and gave her a hug.

Penny was so surprised, she just stood there. Over Season's shoulder, her eyes collided with Quinn's.

She quickly looked away.

Season had already ended the hug, but left her arm around Penny as she walked with her out onto the porch. "You should go next door to the office and say hello to everyone," she encouraged. "David often tells me how patients still ask where you are."

Ordinarily, Penny wouldn't mind hearing that. "I have to get back to Weaver," she murmured. "Otherwise I would." Quinn was standing in the doorway behind Season. He was head and shoulders taller than his mother. He'd folded his arms across his chest, which seemed to make his shoulders look even wider.

Wearing fatigues the way he was, he could have been a picture for a recruiting poster.

"Take care," she told Season and quickly skipped down the porch steps.

But she knew by the prickling in her neck that somebody was following her.

Quinn. He was carrying the unwieldy cardboard and cushion wrap in his arms.

She tried ignoring him as she headed to her car. But sighed when she saw a long slice of the plastic wrapping fall loose behind him.

She caught it before it could blow away, and ended up following him across the street.

He dumped the cardboard into the open-top Dumpster and took the wrap she handed him, tossing it in, as well, over the high side.

She knew she should turn around and get in her car, and get the heck out of Braden. Or at least away from

Quinn. But she couldn't help studying the house on the other side of the Dumpster. "That was my room." She pointed to one of the upper-story windows.

"I know. You liked to sit in the window and read at night."

She looked at him. "Who told you that?"

"Nobody told me. I saw for myself. Because that was my room." He gestured to his parents' house. "When I was here visiting." He lifted his hand and touched the hair hanging over her shoulder. "You'd read and twist your hair." He wound a lock around his index finger. "Like that."

Her heart thumped unevenly in her chest. She stared up at him. He needed a shave again. His jaw was blurred by those dark whiskers that made her fingers itch to touch.

Then he dropped his hand. "I'll be at your house tonight," he said. "Seven."

Her nerve endings jangled at the abruptness. "Why? So you can tell me you're heading back to some godforsaken place where they throw grenades at you? Just tell me now and be done with it. How soon do you go?"

He frowned. "I'm not shipping out. Not yet, anyway."

The level of relief she felt was alarming.

"My leave doesn't end until the end of the month."

So much for relief. "So soon? But what if you're not um, not ready—" What if she wasn't ready?

He didn't answer, though. "I found an attorney to handle the divorce. There's some paperwork involved before we can get started, though. I'll bring it by your house. So be there."

Chapter Ten

"*Answer the phone.*" Holding the phone to her ear, Penny prowled around Margaret Ferguson's apartment. She'd been trying to reach Quinn ever since she'd gotten Margaret's call late that afternoon for help, but had had no luck. And now, if he hadn't left to make the drive to Weaver, he would be soon.

Or he would be late himself for his seven o'clock "be there" edict.

Only Penny wasn't at her house in Weaver.

After returning to Weaver, missing Squire Clay at the diner where his wife had assured Penny he would be, then spending the rest of her afternoon traipsing around town handing out "V is for Vivian" campaign buttons to people who probably just threw them away the second she was out of sight, she'd gotten a call from a frantic Margaret because the babysitter she'd scheduled—Delia Templeton—had canceled at the last minute.

Knowing Margaret was trying to work things out with her estranged husband, Penny hadn't been able to say no. So, for the second time that day, she'd driven back to Braden.

The phone was still ringing. It wasn't even transferring over to a voice mail, which would have been the easiest way to head Quinn and his divorce-related paperwork off at the pass.

Considering his insistence on waiting until they knew for certain that she wasn't pregnant, it felt like he'd all of a sudden gotten into a rush about it.

She blamed it on the fatigues he'd been wearing. Maybe his leave wasn't up yet, but it seemed to her that his mind was already heading that way.

She ended the call and looked down at Matty.

He was sitting on the floor wearing the sandals he'd pulled off her feet, pushing a metal truck around in circles. Penny's concern that he wouldn't be happy being left with her had been for nothing. The toddler had merely welcomed her with a joyful "Bye!" and dumped a load of plastic blocks on her lap that he'd obviously expected her to help stack. When Margaret left a few minutes later, he'd waved, yelling "Bye!" again and again until Penny had distracted him with another toy.

When he saw her looking at him now, he smiled widely, displaying his mouthful of small white teeth. "Book?" He held up his truck.

"That's a truck, Matty. A big, yellow truck."

He pushed off the floor and shuffled in the too-large sandals to the toy bin in the corner. He rummaged inside and pulled out a book, stepped out of her shoes and ran back to shove his new find in her hands. "Book!"

She chuckled, looking at the brightly colored trucks on the front of the board book. "I get it. A book about trucks." She sat down on the floor with her back against the couch and he plopped right onto her lap.

Margaret had just finished giving him his bath when Penny arrived. And now, with his tuft of dark hair leaning against her chest, all Penny could smell was his sweet, baby-clean smell.

The longing that hit her had all the subtlety of a big yellow truck broadsiding her.

She exhaled and reached for her cell phone again. She hit redial while Matty flipped the pages and chortled over the pictures in his sweet, little-boy voice and Penny reminded herself that she wasn't one of those uncontrollable women who couldn't resist hugging and kissing every baby they ever saw.

But Matty wasn't every baby. He was just the one she was watching now. And she nuzzled a quick kiss onto the top of his soft hair.

"Answer the phone," she murmured as she put the phone to her ear.

"Okay." Quinn's voice greeted her and it startled her so much, she dropped the phone altogether. It bounced off the edge of the couch she was leaning against and noisily hit Matty's metal truck before she finally caught it. She fumbled with it and pressed it back to her ear.

"Quinn?"

"What're you doing there?"

"Sorry about that. I dropped the phone." She pushed the truck out of the danger zone and Matty immediately leaned forward to grab it and roll it right back where it had been, all the while making *vroom, vroom* sounds.

Then he looked up at her with his beatific smile. "Book," he yelled exuberantly.

Penny couldn't help smiling. She opened the book and held it out to him. "Read your book, sweetie."

"Read *your* book, sweetie," Quinn said in her ear. "Are you already entertaining my replacement?"

Who could replace Quinn? She shook off the thought.

"Yes," she told him lightly. "He's about three feet tall and has almost all of his teeth."

"Sounds serious."

"Byc!" Matty yelled at the top of his lungs. He tried to grab for the phone, but she angled it out of his reach.

"It's very serious," Penny told Quinn. "I'm considering running away with him. But I think his mama would probably miss him."

"Where *are* you?" She could hear the amusement in his voice.

"Babysitting for a friend," she told him. Matty had turned his attention to the truck yet again and was pushing it around the living area on his hands and knees, so she moved from the floor to the couch. "In Braden. That's why I was calling. I didn't want you driving all the way to Weaver just because of me." She decided she didn't like the way that sounded. "I mean, I know you have plenty of other reasons to go to Weaver, but—"

"I know what you mean. So where exactly are you?"

"I told you. I'm in Braden. We can, uh, can do the paperwork later, right?"

"I'll bring it over. *Where* in Braden?"

She switched hands on the phone and gently rolled back the small red ball that Matty had unearthed from the toy box and inexpertly tossed to her. Quinn's insistence made her nerves tighten. "You don't care anymore whether or not I'm…with child?"

He was silent for a beat. "*Are* you?"

She rubbed her forehead between her eyes. Since Las Vegas, she'd been losing her mind. "My period's due today! Tomorrow at the latest." Her frustration sounded loud and clear. "I should just take a test and clear up your doubt once and for all. Because I am never late. Never."

"If you take a pregnancy test too early, you're going to get a negative result no matter what." His voice was annoyingly reasonable considering everything. "We've waited this long. A few more days won't hurt. Just tell me where you and the three-foot Casanova are at."

She exhaled. Grudgingly told him the address of the apartment.

"I'll be there soon." He hung up.

"Mr. Jump-outta-planes is in a rush," she told Matty.

He grinned and told her what he thought of that. She reached out and tickled his tummy through his "Perfect #1 Son" T-shirt and he bent in half, chortling wildly.

The perfection lasted another hour.

Then sweet, cheerful and friendly Matty turned into screaming, miserable and *un*friendly Matty. Who wanted nothing to do with Penny no matter what she tried. He just wanted his mommy.

Feeling like the worst person on the planet, she'd finally called Margaret. "He's always like that before bedtime," she'd said. "Just put him in his bed and he'll be fine in a few minutes."

"Sure," Penny muttered after discovering that Matty was entirely adept at escaping from his bed. All he'd had to do was magically push the crib a foot away from where it stood until he could reach the dresser and pull out a drawer that he then used as leverage to climb over the side of his crib.

Penny wouldn't have believed it if she hadn't seen it through her own eyes on the baby monitor video.

"A few minutes on what planet?" She huffed her hair out of her eyes and picked up the screaming boy, who mercifully didn't arch his back and shove away from her the way he'd been doing. She carried him into the kitchen. Tried offering him his cartoon-character cup filled with water.

He stopped wailing at least. But after a tiny sip, he just stared at her with huge crocodile tears in his eyes and a pushed-out lip on which a bird could have landed.

Then the doorbell rang.

He started wailing again and with the strength that only an agile two-year-old possessed, wriggled out of her hold. "Mamaaaaaa!" He raced through the living area toward the door.

Even though it had a lock well out of his reach, Penny darted after him. After the crib incident, she knew better than to underestimate the tot's inventiveness. She grabbed him from behind and swung him up in her arms as she peered through the peephole in the door.

Quinn.

Of course it would be Quinn. Not Margaret, coming back to rescue Penny from the demon child.

And what better time could there be to fill out divorce paperwork than when Matty was screaming bloody murder at her?

She flipped open the lock and pulled open the door. "Welcome to—" she considered her miniature audience "—H-E-Double Toothpicks."

At the sight of Quinn, though, Matty's screaming stopped midbreath. His eyes widened as he looked up, and then up some more until he got to Quinn's face.

"Hey, bud." Quinn held out his palm. "What's doing?"

Matty slapped his palm against Quinn's. "Sssdoing!" He still had tears on his sweaty cheeks but one look at Quinn—still in his damned camo—and life was good again.

"Clearly, it's true that all males stick together," she said grumpily. She turned away from the door. "Come on in to the mad, mad world of Matty the Great. Watch your step, though. Over the last hour, he's tossed every toy out of his toy box and refuses to let me put any of them back. It's like walking through a minefield."

Quinn laughed softly. "Honey, I've been through real minefields. This is nothing."

She didn't need a reminder about his real work. The research she'd done online about it was more than enough to keep her awake at night. Not only had she read voraciously about pararescue in general, she'd found a photo of him looking ungodly handsome in his dress uniform when he'd received his Silver Star. And she'd read the account of the bombing in which he'd been injured.

Quinn was a hero in every sense of the word. Saving lives was in his blood, even when it meant putting his own in peril.

She went to set Matty on the floor, but in typical toddler contrariness, he suddenly clung tenaciously to her neck. She straightened and he put his head on her shoulder and popped his thumb in his mouth.

An angel, once again.

The thumb, though, was a good enough sign for her. "I'm going to try to put him to bed again." She glanced over the decimation of the living area. One of the couch cushions was on the floor and the rest of them were misaligned. Every other surface seemed to be home to one of Matty's seemingly endless supply of toys. "I'd say make yourself comfortable, but I'm not sure where that would be."

There was a smile in his eyes. It extended to the ray of fine lines beside them. But he didn't say a word. Just looked at her for a moment that seemed to stretch until she finally huffed a little. *"What?"*

He took a step forward and cupped his hand behind her neck and kissed her softly.

She went stock-still, hardly able to conceive a single thought as shock and giddiness and heat blasted through her.

The recording of their wedding kiss flitted through her mind but disintegrated in a puff when, just as unexpectedly, he lifted his head and stepped back again.

All told, it was more of a peck than a real kiss, but it still left her scrambling for composure. "What the he— heck was that for?"

"'Cause you're just too damn cute for words."

Even more disconcerted, she gave him a fierce frown. *Cute* was not a word she particularly welcomed. Combined with the stupid *giddiness*, it made her feel as mature as a teenager. "I'm not cute," she muttered as she turned on her heel and carried Matty into his bedroom.

His head was still on her shoulder. She stood next to his crib, swaying with him for a few minutes and humming in her off-key way that he didn't seem to mind too much as she surreptitiously felt his diaper. Fortunately, it was still dry because she'd learned right off that changing Matty's diaper meant chasing a bare-butt Matty around the apartment while trying to get him back into a dry one.

He gave a ferocious sigh and patted her face as she gingerly lowered him into the crib. "Night night, sweetheart."

His thumb went back into his mouth and he turned onto his stomach, his diaper-covered butt going into the air.

It was silly. But her eyes suddenly flooded.

She snatched a tissue from the box on Matty's dresser and wiped her eyes. Her nose. Then she shoved the crumpled tissue into the pocket of her jeans and tugged up the strap of her black tank top and went out to face Quinn.

He'd restored the cushions to proper order and was sitting in the middle of the couch.

Only then did she remember the baby monitor. It had been sitting on the table next to the couch and Quinn had obviously discovered it, since he was holding it in his hands.

She sincerely hoped he hadn't noticed the whole teary-eyed thing.

"You ever think about having kids?"

So much for *that* hope. But at least he hadn't made a big deal about her sniffling.

As a girl, she'd thought about having Andy's kids. But it had always been in terms of finally having a real family of her own.

Now was the first time she was really thinking about a *child*. The reality of one. The confounding blessing and responsibility and maybe even the need of one.

She chewed the inside of her cheek, buying time by picking up a handful of toys and carefully placing them back in the toy box for fear that one of them would bust into noisy song and wake up Matty again.

"I never thought about it," he finally said into the silence. "Not until—"

"Las Vegas," she finished, sending him a look.

"No."

Surprised, she straightened.

He pressed his hand to his side where she knew his scars were. "When I woke up after this and knew I wasn't dead, I thought about kids. I thought about a lot of stuff that I had put aside because of the choices I've made in my life."

Her chest felt tight. She had that ominous burning behind her eyes again, but fiercely ignored it. "From the looks of you, your choices haven't changed."

"What's that supposed to mean?"

She waved her hand at him. "You look ready to report for duty. What do they say? The clothes make the man?" Even as she said it, though, she knew that wasn't the case where Quinn Templeton was concerned. He could be naked or dressed in a joker's costume and he'd still be exactly who he was. A man who'd put his own life in danger over and over for the sake of someone else.

He plucked at his pants. "Penny, sometimes a pair of digies is just a pair of digies." He smiled gently. "Particularly when everything else I have with me needs to be washed. That's what I was doing at my folks' house this morning. Hitting up my mother for some laundry duty."

"You're a grown man. You should do your own laundry."

"And I do. Often. But it was Mom or a laundromat since my cousin doesn't know what a washing machine even is." He held out his hand to her. "Come here."

She eyed his hand. Long, square-tipped fingers. Broad, square-shaped palm. Putting her hand in his seemed dangerous. Like she'd be taking a step into a land in which she was afraid to live.

And sometimes a hand is just a hand.

Her eyes burned again and she ignored his outstretched palm as she went over and sat next to him on the couch. Considering his hogging the middle of the thing, that left her with the choice of a half a cushion on one side of him or half a cushion on the other. "So where's the paperwork?"

He seemed to sigh. Then he pulled a folded envelope out of his back pocket and extracted several pages. "We have to decide which one of us is filing. I'm domiciled in Wyoming, and obviously I know you've lived here for more than sixty days."

"My whole life. I was born at the Weaver hospital." She felt his gaze.

"Me, too," he murmured. He pointed at the boxes printed on the form and his shoulder brushed against hers. "So either one of us can be the petitioner." He went silent.

Was he waiting for her to say something?

But what? Yes, she wanted to be the one to divorce him? No, she didn't?

"This is weird," she admitted huskily as she scanned through the form. "Deciding these things about a divorce when we don't even feel married." Birthdate. Previous marriages. Children born during the current marriage.

Was petitioner pregnant?

She swallowed hard at that one.

"You don't have to decide anything right now," he said.

Not deciding something that should be so simple seemed like it was a decision, too.

A noise from the baby monitor made her jump.

Quinn picked up the monitor and held it where they could both see. Even though Penny had turned off the light in Matty's room, the black-and-white image was clear, showing him sitting up in his crib, rubbing his eyes.

She held her breath.

He made a few squawks, then rolled over again, butt in the air, and silence reigned once more.

She blew out a relieved breath.

"You didn't answer before." Quinn's thumb rubbed over the monitor's screen. Almost like he was rubbing little Matty's back.

She looked up at him. Her heart climbed inexorably until she felt it pounding hard at the base of her throat.

She realized she was looking at his mouth and quickly lifted her gaze to his. But that was really no safer. "About what?"

"About having kids." His deep voice seemed to drop a notch. "You ever think about it?"

She tried to look away. But her disobedient eyes only went as far as his mouth.

His beautiful, perfectly molded lips that set off long-forgotten dreams whenever they touched hers.

She pushed off the couch and winced when her bare foot landed on a connecting block. She flicked it free and started putting more toys away. An airplane with a nose that blinked orange and announced robotically "now boarding" as soon as she touched it. A play cell phone that noisily buzzed until she shoved it under one of the couch cushions.

"I didn't know toys made so many noises these days." She smiled weakly and went to grab the red ball. That, at least, didn't sing or talk or chirp or buzz.

"Penny."

She dropped the ball into the toy box and bent over to grab the book about trucks.

"What are you so afraid of?"

She managed what she thought was a credible amount of offense. "I'm not afraid of anything."

"Then sit here. *Talk* to me."

Wasn't it supposed to be a woman's lament that the man in her life never wanted to talk?

Since when is Quinn the man *in your life?*

He's my husband, isn't he?

She thought she might well be losing her mind as the argument raged inside her. "This is all your fault," she accused, pointing at him with the book.

Instead of defending himself, though, he just looked

at her with those beautiful, dark eyes. So solemn. So serious. "I know. I should have done a better job protecting you."

"I don't need your protection!" Frustration bubbled in her veins. She threw out her arms. "I don't want to feel this way!"

His brows pulled together slightly. He leaned forward, resting his arms on his knees. His palms turned upward. "What way?"

Stymied, she flopped her arms down to her sides and paced to the toy box. She dropped the truck book inside and scooped up a headless, naked baby doll by the arm. "We'd both better hope I'm not pregnant. Because you know what I know about kids?" She shook the headless doll at him. "Nothing." She dropped it into the toy box.

"You worked at my father's practice for ten years."

"I handled supplies and billing," she dismissed. It was a gross understatement and she knew it. "Not the children."

"Right. None of those kids who still ask about where you are."

She grimaced. She stared down at the poor, bedraggled baby doll body. "How can I think about having a baby—" *Quinn's baby* "—when I can't even remember *making* one?"

"You want a refresher?"

She gaped at him.

"Don't look so shocked. God knows I'm willing." His eyes roved over, suddenly full of heat.

Tempting heat.

"And I can be pretty persuasive," he added with a devilish smile.

Warmth was blooming inside her. The problem was that he wouldn't have to work hard at persuading. At all.

"I'm not having…having *sex* with you just because I can't remember having sex with you!"

His lips twitched. "I might be a little wounded by that if it didn't sound so funny."

"Nothing about this is funny."

He stood and came over to her, trapping her between his big, tall body and the toy box behind her legs. He closed his hands around her arms and squeezed lightly. "Look at it this way." He smiled wryly. "It's been a couple weeks. You say you're never late. So you'll get your period today or tomorrow and you can choose to look at it as just a night of forgettable sex. Literally."

"My only night of forgettable sex," she grumbled, too determined to resist being coaxed out of her funk to think about what she was saying. "My only night of sex, more like."

She felt the change in his grip. One second, easy and light. The next second, not.

"What do you mean, your *only* night of sex?"

Chapter Eleven

"Penny?" Quinn tightened his grip on her arms when she didn't answer. But the tide of red creeping up her neck was all the answer he needed. "Are you saying you're a virgin?"

Her eyes skated away from his. "I think *was* is more applicable."

Realization was setting in. And anger. Squarely aimed at himself. "Why the hell didn't you say something?"

That got her blue eyes focused on his face again. "Because it's such an easy thing to work into a conversation? Oh, by the way, Quinn," she said in a mocking tone, "while you're stirring your cup of tea there, don't you think it's just hilarious that I *finally* had sex and can't remember a single second of it?"

He ignored the sarcasm. "You were engaged." He couldn't fathom any red-blooded young man not wanting to jump the gun on that score.

Her eyebrows went up. "I told you there were strict rules living with the Bennetts. What do you think would have happened if Andy and I had been caught having sex? We'd have both been yanked right out of that foster home and placed elsewhere. Placed God knows where. We might have ended up in different towns, even! There wasn't anything worth taking the chance of being separated."

It was hard to believe. "Once Andy turned eighteen? What was the danger then?"

Her jaw worked. Her cheeks were red. "He wanted to wait until we were married. So we waited. You don't know what it was like," she said defensively. Her words came faster, like she'd tumbled over a hill and was picking up speed. "For kids like us. Andy's mom was a prostitute. She lost him when he was eight. Before the Bennetts, he landed for a few years with a minister and his wife. He learned the Bible. He learned about being *good*. But then Mr. and Mrs. Minister had a baby girl of their own. So they suddenly didn't have room for him. Not the boy whose mom was a sex-addicted hooker.

"So he got shipped to the next place. And the next until he finally got to the Bennetts. To me." Her eyes shimmered. "But he never got mean like some did. And he never got angry. He just said we could wait until everything was legal and right and nobody could take us away from each other." Her voice went hoarse. "Ever."

She was killing him.

He closed his arms around her and pulled her against him.

Her fists thumped his back. "It wasn't *fair*."

"No. It wasn't fair."

"I would have been a good wife."

He closed his eyes and pressed his cheek against the

top of her head. There was no competing against a dead man. Particularly one who'd apparently been half saint when he'd lived. "I know."

Her hands stopped thumping. She gave a deep shuddering sigh, resting her head against his chest. He could feel her heartbeat.

"I'll be a better mom than my mom was," she finally said huskily. "You know. If and when."

His eyes stung. "Yeah. I know."

She pulled back and looked up at him with an expression he couldn't read. Then suddenly, she stretched up, wrapped her arms around his neck and pressed her mouth to his.

Sparks zinged straight down his spine, flaming the fire banked inside him. As easy as it would be to let it burn; as much as he wanted to let it burn, he couldn't. Not now. Not when she still had tears on her cheeks from grief over someone else. And not when she might as well still be a virgin—emotionally if not physically.

Even if she was pregnant with his baby.

The irony was almost too much to stomach.

He gently pulled her clinging hands from his neck. Reluctantly pulled his mouth away from hers.

Her luminous eyes had darkened. From aquamarine to sapphire. And no less disturbing. "Well." Her voice was tight. "This seems familiar."

He knew she wasn't talking about that night two weeks ago. She was talking about that night nearly fifteen years ago. Before Andy. "You were a kid." And a hell of a temptation despite that fact. "And I could've landed my ass in jail if I'd taken what you were trying to offer."

"Everything is entirely proper now." Her voice was tight. "Lawfully wedded and everything."

"And you're as off-limits as ever."

She swiped her hand over her cheeks, pulling away from him. "Don't make excuses, Quinn. It doesn't suit you."

He slapped down a backdraft of anger. "It's not an excuse. It's a fact. You think I don't want you? You think that was an aberration, waking up like we did in Las Vegas?" He grabbed her forearms and pulled her against him, feeling her shocked *oomph* when he slid his hands around her hips and hauled her even closer. So she would have no more doubt about that particular fact.

Her lips parted.

"Yeah," he said through his teeth. "I *want*. And now, there's no way I can *have*." He let go of her and stepped away, automatically avoiding the brightly colored stacking blocks in his path. "If it weren't for that night that neither one of us can remember, you'd still *be* a virgin." It wasn't entirely true that he didn't remember that night. He remembered the wedding. He remembered getting back to the hotel. To his room.

The memories had been haunting his sleep since they'd started recurring. Remembering the taste of her mouth as it opened under his. The feel of her skin as he'd pulled away her dress.

Her cheeks had gone red again. But there was no way to get through this mess without stating the facts, whether she was embarrassed by them or not.

"If I'm still a virgin, at least that would be grounds for an annulment." Her tone was flippant.

He exhaled roughly, raking his fingers through his hair. His gaze fell on the lawyer's paperwork. They'd been more of an excuse to see Penny than a burning desire to get going on the undoing of their Vegas "do's." Particularly when he wasn't certain he wanted to undo anything.

Penny hadn't known where he'd been over the last several days. No one did. He'd been in the Tetons hauling backpacks loaded down with sandbags to mimic the weight of the rucks he wore on a mission and enough water to keep from getting dehydrated. He'd rock-climbed. He'd rappelled. He'd hiked until he couldn't distinguish the pain of his healed injuries from the pain everywhere else.

And he'd sat on a ridge where it was easy to imagine no human had ever sat, and he'd watched the sun come up over some of the most beautiful land he'd seen around the globe.

He still didn't know what he was going to do when his leave was up. Continue fighting to regain his flight status when he had his exam with the flight surgeon in a few weeks, or take the promotion he'd been offered and the desk that came along with it?

But he knew he didn't want to go back without at least exploring this *thing* that hung between him and Penny. It wasn't just the wedding business. And it wasn't just the fact that he couldn't close his eyes without imagining her against him. Beneath him. Over him.

It was something else.

Something that was a damn sight more disturbing.

Something that was making him seriously consider what he wanted his future to look like, regardless of how well things went with the flight surgeon.

The noise from the baby monitor sounded loud. Penny jumped. He was a little more battle-hardened to sudden and unexpected noise.

She snatched up the monitor, though, with the fervor of a drowning person.

"You can hold on to the paperwork," he said, heading

to the door. "Figure out what you want to do about it. I'll be in touch. And Penny—"

She gave him a wary look. "What?"

"Just for the record, I'm not hoping that you're not pregnant." Technically, that should mean that he was hoping she *was*, which he wasn't quite ready to admit, either.

Her lips parted. He'd obviously shocked her.

But if he'd hoped that she would convey a similar feeling, he was headed for disappointment.

A wail suddenly reverberated through the apartment as well as the monitor, causing an echoing effect.

"I, uh, I'd better check on Matty." She started to leave the room. But stopped. "I'll call you, if, um, if—"

"There's any reason to call?"

Her lips twisted. She nodded once before hurrying out of the room.

Quinn exhaled. He looked over the mess of toys still scattered everywhere. Then he let himself out the front door, turning the lock so it would latch behind him.

Four days later Penny chewed the inside of her lip as she studied the store shelf. There were pink boxes. There were blue boxes. Purple ones. White ones. Name brands. Store brands.

Five tests in a box. Two tests in a box.

She plucked a large box of Stork Strips off the shelf just out of sheer disbelief. "Twenty test strips?" As far as she was concerned, whoever needed that many pregnancy tests was really living on the edge.

"Penny. Is that you?"

She shoved the box back on the shelf when she heard her name and looked over to see a pretty blonde approaching.

She stifled her frustration. It was ten o'clock on a

Tuesday morning. She'd thought it would be a safe time to make a run into Shop-World and purchase a test kit when the store was notoriously slow. But she'd already run into Bubba Bumble, and then Josh McArthur and his wife. And now, one of Vivian's granddaughters?

Didn't anyone have to work in this town?

She reached above the shelf of pregnancy tests and grabbed a box of tampons, as if that was what she'd been standing there in that aisle to choose all along. "Hi, Hayley." She dropped the box into her cart.

A needless box, since her period was still MIA.

Ergo her furtive attempt to select a dang pregnancy test without someone she knew seeing. Along with tampons she didn't need, she also had a twelve-pack of toilet paper and two rolls of paper towels that she didn't need. The oversize bottle of pain reliever, though?

She was beginning to think that would come in handy.

Obviously, it wasn't going to be a quick hello-how-are-you as they passed in the aisle. "How's your summer going?"

Hayley smiled but her gaze slid to the shelves of blue, pink and purple boxes and Penny willed herself not to blush.

"It's good." Hayley tucked a long strand of hair behind her ear. "I heard about my grandmother's trip to Pennsylvania last week."

Penny could well imagine. Carter Templeton was Hayley's father. And after he'd seen his mother's gift of the portrait, he'd called Vivian to rail at her tactics. He didn't appreciate her thinking she'd have to bribe him to want a portrait of his own father.

Unfortunately, since Vivian had refused to take the telephone, Penny had been on the listening end of the man's tirade.

"It was an interesting trip, that's for sure. I've never seen a mansion like that. Outside of television or the movies, I mean."

"You're one up on me. I've never been there at all. Seth tells me that we should go before Grandmother sells it. But with his work schedule at Cee-Vid and my patient load, I don't know when we'd fit it in. We had dinner with her last night. Sounds like she's expecting an offer on it any day."

Penny didn't know if it was her paranoia or not that made it seem like Hayley was intentionally lingering there. Vivian was particularly close to Hayley. But Vivian wouldn't have told Hayley about Penny and Quinn.

Would she?

And even though Vivian knew about the wedding, she couldn't possibly know about the rest.

"Anyway…" Hayley finally plucked a bottle of deodorant off a low shelf and dropped it into the handbasket she was carrying over her elbow. "It was good to see you."

Penny smiled. "You, too." She pushed her cart around to the next aisle while Hayley slowly headed the other way.

She hoped Hayley left soon. Penny was due to pick up Vivian from the hairdresser in less than a half hour. The rest of their day was already filled, and that evening Penny was planning to stake out Colbys Bar & Grill for a chance to corner Squire Clay about the debate. After missing him the other day, his wife had given Penny fresh intel.

Feeling the time ticking away, she hovered there in the dog and cat food aisle, even though she had no such dog and no such cat. After what felt like ample time for Hayley to have vacated the danger zone, she pushed her cart back around the corner.

But Hayley had gone right back to where they'd been. She was looking at that same 20-stripper box of Stork Strips.

Consternated, Penny started to back away with the cart, but Hayley spotted her before she could, giving her own startled jump. Then she flushed and held up the box. "You caught me," she said with a chagrined smile. "Who would need *twenty* tests?"

"Somebody who is having a lot of sex," Penny managed wryly.

Hayley chuckled. "Whoever it is, obviously there's a market for it, or it wouldn't be here on the shelf at Shop-World." She made a face, then gave a sort of "oh-well" shrug before snatching a pink box and placing it into her basket.

Penny had been so self-involved that it took her a moment. She had such a beleaguered conscience that she hadn't even considered Hayley would have her own reason for being in that shopping aisle. "Oh. Wow. Congratulations."

"Well..." Hayley lifted her slender shoulder. "That remains to be seen. But Seth and I are hopeful." She switched the basket to her other arm. "You won't tell anyone, will you? If it's positive, we want to make a proper announcement."

"Of course!" Penny mimicked locking her lips. "No worries on that score."

"Thanks." Hayley glanced at the narrow watch on her wrist. "Shoot. I'm really running late now." She turned on her heel with a wave. "Thanks again, Penny."

Hayley wasn't the only one running late.

Penny gave a last glance at the test kits stacked so neatly and so colorfully, and turned her cart around to head for the exit. She found a clerk on her way and apologized for the stuff in her cart that would need to be restocked, because she didn't have time to stand in the checkout line and still be on time picking up Vivian.

"Nobody apologizes for that," the clerk said with a smile. He took the cart and rolled it away as Penny headed for the exit. She saw Hayley standing in line and sent her a thumbs-up before hurrying out to the parking lot and the Rolls Royce.

She'd parked it way off in a far corner of the lot where no one was likely to park nearby and possibly door-ding the expensive vehicle.

So, given her luck lately, naturally there was a big dusty pickup parked right next to it.

"Now *why*?" she asked under her breath as she quickly crossed the lot that had ample spaces still available. "All the spots and you choose that one?"

She hitched the strap of her purse higher over her shoulder as she rounded the vehicle to the driver's side. When she did, the door of the pickup opened and Quinn got out.

Her nerves rear-ended each other as they screeched to a halt. "What are you doing here?"

"I told you I'd be in touch."

"Yeah, last Friday." Her gaze roved over him like they were starved for the sight. At least he wasn't wearing the camouflage pants. "Digies," as he'd called them, though she had no idea why. Now he had on a pair of blue jeans and a plain white T-shirt that some long-ago genius had designed with Quinn in mind.

He wasn't hoping that she wasn't pregnant.

She pushed aside his admission the same way she'd been pushing it aside since he'd made it.

"And how'd you know where I was, anyway?" She hadn't told anyone she planned to stop at Shop-World.

"I didn't." He nodded pointedly toward the car. "But there's only one Phantom in these parts. And as much as my granny Viv is trying to fit into the community with her *modestly* sized house—" his voice was dry "—and her run for town council, I just can't see either her or Montrose shopping at Shop-World. Which left *you*." His gaze ran over her clearly empty hands. "Didn't find what you came to buy?"

She shook her head, looking down at her feet until she thought the threat of blushing was past. "I, ah, I came to buy a—" This was humiliating. And it shouldn't be. She was officially thirty years old as of that day. It was a perfectly reasonable age to be a sexually active adult.

An annoying snicker whispered in the back of her mind. *Too bad you can't remember the* activity.

She lifted her head. "A pregnancy test," she blurted. Why not? She still had an unopened box of condoms dwelling at the bottom of her purse. "I came to buy a pregnancy test. There. You satisfied?"

He looked a lot calmer about it than she felt. "Okay. Let's do the test. Right now."

She was afraid her eyebrows might shoot right off her forehead. "What would you like me to do? Tinkle on the stick behind your truck? I can't, anyway. I didn't get one purchased."

"Why not?"

"Because I kept running into people I knew!" All the exasperation she felt came out in the admission.

But Quinn just looked like he was trying not to smile.

Which was even more exasperating, because there was nothing remotely funny about the situation.

"Don't you laugh," she warned.

"Wouldn't dream of it," he assured blithely. He looked past her toward the big-box store. "I'll go in and get one," he said. "Any particular brand impress you more than the others?"

"The twenty-stripper," she said without thought. Of course he wouldn't be squeamish about buying the kit. He was so comfortable in who he was, he could probably buy a warehouse full of feminine products in front of God and country and not turn a dark hair on his infernally handsome head.

"What's a twenty-stripper?"

"Never mind. Get um—" she thought of the box that Hayley Banyon had chosen "—the pink box." She refused to buy something called Stork Sticks. "I don't know what it's called. The names were just a blur to me. But there was a picture of two test sticks on the front." Just in case she somehow managed to screw up the first one and needed a backup.

Given her luck these days, anything was possible.

"Sit tight and I'll be right back." He started to step around her.

"Wait!"

He stopped, looking down at her.

She unaccountably felt breathless.

"I mean, uh, I can't…can't wait."

His eyebrow went up. She had the strangest notion that he was looking at her lips, and her mouth went dry. She didn't even realize how close they were standing until a horn honking nearby startled them.

"I have to pick up your grandmother from the, uh, the hairdresser," she finished so huskily that she flushed.

He softly cleared his throat. "Then I'll bring it to her place."

She swallowed. "I can't do the test there," she protested weakly.

He smiled again, just slightly, then made her shiver

when he brushed his thumb down her cheek. "Sweetheart, you can do the test anywhere you can take a leak."

Sweetheart. It was just a word. It meant nothing.

Riiiight.

There was another honk and, blinking, she looked past him to see an impatient driver waiting behind another car to exit the parking lot.

She looked back at Quinn and resolutely stiffened her shoulders against his appeal. "Not your grandmother's." She reeled off Vivian's busy schedule that was also going to keep Penny busy for the rest of the day. "And tonight, I need to corner Squire Clay once and for all about doing the debate. The only place it can logically be held is in Weaver's high school auditorium and if I'm going to get it reserved in time, I need to make the commitment."

"So make the commitment. If the debate never comes off, Vivian's got plenty of money to cover the inconvenience."

"Yes, but it's not only money. School will be starting and they have their own activities that need to be shuffled around to accommodate the debate. If it doesn't end up happening and Vivian put them through that work, it'll damage her in the polls."

His eyebrows rose. "Weaver has election polls where town council seats are concerned?"

She grimaced. "You know what I mean. Reputation is everything around here."

"Well, that's true enough," he agreed wryly. He opened the driver's door of Vivian's fancy car for her. "So go on and get her from the hairdresser. I'll buy the test and catch up to you later sometime."

"I'll be at Colbys," she warned as she got behind the wheel of the car. "In case you don't find me at home. You know where Colbys is, right?"

He gave her a look. "Weaver being such a metropolis and all? Yeah, I know where it's located." He pulled out the safety belt next to her shoulder and waited until she took the buckle.

Something inside her chest felt hot as their fingers brushed, and she fumbled with fitting the latch into place.

Then he pushed the door closed between them and headed toward the store.

She couldn't tear her gaze away from his departing form until the *ping* on her phone reminded her that she was supposed to be picking up Vivian on the other side of town.

She exhaled shakily and drove slowly out of the lot. The last thing she needed to do was have an accident in the fancy car because she was having crazy fantasies about the man she'd married.

Chapter Twelve

Even on a Tuesday night, Colbys Bar & Grill was doing a brisk business. The parking on the street in front of the building was full and the lot on the side was just as bad. The closest spot Penny found was nearly two blocks away.

After finally leaving Vivian for the day, Penny had raced home—half afraid, half incomprehensibly excited—to see if Quinn had left the pregnancy kit there for her.

But there'd been no sign of him. No brown paper bag sitting on her porch. No pink box waiting anywhere.

What had been waiting, though, had been her mail.

The sight of the bright pink birthday card wasn't unusual.

Susie Bennett had been mailing them to Penny every year since she and George had moved away. The fact that the handwritten address on the front of the envelope was correct meant that Susie had kept up with Penny's whereabouts from someone.

Dr. T? His wife?

Penny hadn't had an answer and rather than deal with her feelings about it, she'd shoved the card in her lingerie chest where all the other unopened cards sat alongside Quinn's paperwork from the lawyer that was still untouched and incomplete.

Then, because for the first time since she'd accompanied Vivian to Pennsylvania, she'd found herself with a little spare time on her hands, she'd taken a longer-than-usual shower. Taken the time to blow-dry her hair smooth for once. She'd put on makeup. Real makeup. Not just a smear of tinted balm on her lips. Dressed in a newish pair of blue jeans that still held most of their indigo blue, and a sapphire-colored T-shirt.

She'd told herself it was only because she wanted to blend in at Colbys.

As a lie to herself, it was a pretty thin one. The usual dress code at the bar was that there was no dress code. In the times she'd been there, that meant anything sufficed. From mudcaked jeans and cowboy boots to the occasional miniskirt.

The last miniskirt Penny had worn had been black and covered with sequins that Susie Bennett had taught her to sew on by hand. She'd worn it to the Sadie Hawkins' Day dance when Andy had come back for two days after his basic training.

When she thought about the tight spit of fabric, she still couldn't believe that Susie had allowed it.

The skirt was still lying in the bottom of one of her dresser drawers.

She hadn't let herself think about the Bennetts for so many years. And now every time she turned around, she was confronted with memories of them.

She'd reached the entrance to Colbys and she took a deep breath before pulling it open.

The second she stepped inside, she was engulfed in noise.

The clacking of balls on the collection of pool tables arranged to one side of the bar. The sound of Garth Brooks singing about if tomorrow never came and the underlying clamor of voices, laughter and the thunk of bottles and clatter of dishes.

She spotted Squire Clay immediately. The old man had a full, distinctive head of iron-gray hair and stood tall despite the gnarled walking stick he had clutched in his fist. Considering the way he was waving that stick in the air as he was watching the action going on at one of the pool tables, she wondered if he needed it for walking at all.

"Dammit, Jefferson," she could hear him yell as she headed his way, "didn't I teach you better 'n that? Gonna let a little slip of a thing like our Meggie beat you at pool? You're getting old, son!"

Penny caught the wry expression on Jefferson Clay's face as he ignored his father's haranguing. She'd only met Jefferson once—at the lavish Christmas party Vivian had thrown.

She'd worked for Vivian for only a few months at that point. Now, after months of gaining a deeper understanding of Vivian and the estrangement she'd had with her sons, not to mention seeing those paintings of Sawyer Templeton, Penny was starting to see some resemblances between Squire's offspring with his first wife and Vivian's offspring with her first husband. Physical and otherwise.

Squire had mercifully stopped waving around his cane when Penny stood next to him. She was glad she'd chosen to wear her good cowboy boots that added a couple inches to her height, because it put her pretty close to looking the cagey old rancher in the eye. "Mr. Clay? Pardon me for intruding on your evening. I'm Penny Garner." She hitched her purse higher on her shoulder and stuck out her hand because she was pretty certain that he was too old school to just ignore her.

His eyes were such a pale shade of blue they almost looked as silvery as his hair. And as they narrowed as he looked at her, she felt the same hint of nervousness she'd felt when she'd first gone to work for Vivian.

Then his lips compressed and he shook her hand briefly. "Miz Garner. Hope you're here for grub or suds. Otherwise I'm gonna start thinking you're not real quick on the uptake."

"Don't be rude, Squire." A graying auburn-haired woman stepped forward. Penny knew, even before she found her hand warmly clasped, that the woman had to be Squire's wife, Gloria. "Penny's been nothing but charming whenever we've spoken." Gloria gave her a quick wink.

Squire harrumphed. "Should've known you'd be manipulating things behind my back."

Gloria was clearly unperturbed by the accusation. "Since you're being your usual cantankerous self, someone has to take on the dirty task."

"Jefferson," Squire barked. "You gonna let that girl beat you *again*?"

"That girl," Jefferson drawled as he set down his pool cue and shoved his fingers through the thick blond hair that hung past his shoulders, "is a shark who has been taught well by another shark. *You*."

Squire let out a satisfied cackle as he shared a look with the beaming teenager standing on the other side of the pool table. "Damn straight." He looked from the teen to Penny. "You're a good-looking thing," he said. "Wouldn't you rather be home cooking for your husband than dancing to that Templeton woman's tune?"

"Squire," Gloria chided. She looked at Penny. "Take about a third of what he says seriously. The rest of what comes out of his mouth is purely for effect."

Penny sure hoped so. "Mr. Clay, what can I say to convince you to participate in the debate?"

"Not a damn thing, girl." He gave her a sidelong look. "That's no reflection on your efforts, I assure you."

She supposed that was something. "But—"

"There's just no call for a debate." His lip curled with annoyance. "Your *boss* doesn't understand the way we do things here. Weaver *ain't* Pittsburgh."

"But there is a reason for debate," she argued. "It's been more than two decades since there have been more candidates for town council than there are available vacancies! You have an enviable opportunity here. Unlike a lot of small towns, Weaver is thriving. It'll outpace Braden before long at the rate it's growing. Don't you think the citizens deserve to hear what both of the candidates have to say about the future of their community?"

Squire gave her a look. "Sure *you* shouldn't be running for the council yourself?"

She lifted her chin and smiled, feeling unaccountably confident all of a sudden. "If I were the one running against you, would you feel differently about having the debate?"

He harrumphed again and looked past her.

A shiver slid down her spine and she knew that Quinn had entered the bar even before she turned to look.

He stood a head taller than nearly everyone in the crowded room as he made his way toward them and she had the silliest notion of telling Squire that she didn't need to be home cooking for her husband, because her husband was already *there*.

When he reached them, his easy smile took in everyone surrounding the pool table. His white T-shirt from earlier that day had been replaced by a beige button-down with the sleeves rolled up. "Evening." His fingers grazed the small of her spine, warm even through her T-shirt. "Meant to get here sooner, but I got tied up with something."

She felt breathless. And grateful that he wasn't carrying a pink box. She dragged her eyes from the base of his strong neck displayed in the middle of his casually unbuttoned collar. She couldn't seem to get the smile off her face, either. "I... I just got here myself." She gestured. "I think I should probably make some introductions."

Squire interrupted, though. He was eyeing Quinn closely. "You're the young buck with the Silver Star."

Quinn looked surprised. "Can't say I've been called a young buck in a while," he said wryly.

Squire grunted. "You look a lot like your grandpa," he said abruptly.

"I never met him."

"Would'a been hard when he died a long time before you were even born." Squire stuck out his hand. "I'm Squire." He gestured with his other. "Most of those faces over there're your relatives. You're welcome to join us for supper, if you're interested."

Quinn shook the old man's hand and his nod took in all the rest. "I appreciate the offer, sir. But I've actually got plans already with Penny here." His fingertips stroked along Penny's spine again.

Squire's look turned appraising. "Well, can't say you don't have good taste," he said.

Penny felt herself start to flush. "Mr. Clay. About

the debate—" She broke off, startled, when someone screamed. Followed by another scream.

As one, they'd all turned to look.

"What the hell," Squire was muttering. He dropped his hand on Penny's shoulder as he tried to see through the commotion that was suddenly the central focus of the chaotic bar.

Quinn was the first to move. He caught Penny's eyes. "Call 911. You hear me?"

She nodded and quickly pushed through the people who'd started crowding forward toward the bar while he headed into the throng. She could hear his deep voice cutting calmly and authoritatively through the clamor as she reached the bar. Merilee, the assistant manager of the place, already had the phone at her ear, though.

"Call 911!"

Merilee nodded, lifting her hand. "I am! No," she yelled into the phone. "I don't know the nature of my emergency. I just have one! That's right. Colbys. Oh, for God's sake. We only *have* one location. On Main. Near the park."

When Penny had arrived, every bar stool at the bar had been occupied. Now they were all empty. She dumped her purse on the bar and climbed up onto one so she could see above the crowd. Quinn was crouched over a man, obviously giving him CPR.

"A man's not breathing," she told Merilee, who in turn yelled it at the person on the other end of the line.

Merilee slammed down the phone. "Both ambulances are already out. Sheriff's sending a van."

Penny had spotted a distinctive white and red box hanging on the wall behind the bar. She scrambled off the bar stool and darted around the bar to open the metal container. She snatched out the AED and shoved her way through the bodies until she reached Quinn.

"Here." She set the portable defibrillator down beside him. "There's a sheriff van coming, but no ambulance—they're already out on calls," she told him in a low voice as she opened the AED case, thanking her stars that Dr. T had kept all of his staff regularly trained for CPR. She'd done her last refresher course shortly before she'd begun working for Vivian.

She was vaguely aware that Squire's wife had made it through the throng and was crouching down in the crowded space between the close-set tables.

"Nurse," Gloria told them briskly before ordering everyone to take a few steps back.

"Now," Squire barked, slamming the end of his walking stick against a table.

Like everyone else, Penny jumped. Someone was crying loudly and Gloria was trying to calm her. Penny quickly turned on the AED as feet shuffled around them, affording them a little more breathing room. Quinn had stripped back the man's shirt until his chest was bare and he applied the AED pads. Though she'd never seen the machine in real use, she knew it would automatically check for an abnormal heart rhythm.

Quinn, however, was obviously very familiar with the device. "Everyone back," he barked. "Penny, make sure there's a path to the door."

She pushed to her feet just as the AED delivered a shock to the poor man, and stepped carefully around them both.

"Come on," she ordered, clapping her hands for attention as she shouldered her way. "Get these tables moved back. You—" she pointed at one of Colbys waitresses who was probably all of eighteen and looked scared out of her wits as she squarely blocked Penny's way "—help Merilee get as many people to move into the grill as you can." She took the girl's shoulders and turned her toward the grill, which was connected to the bar by a short breezeway. "Go."

Finally, there was some progress in clearing a path. The door on the street had opened and she could see the flashing red and blue light of the sheriff van outside.

It felt like forever to Penny, but as she, too, stepped aside while Quinn and two uniformed officers carried the unconscious victim out, she realized it had really only been a matter of minutes.

She saw Gloria accompanying the crying woman after them and blew out a long breath.

"At least they don't have far to get to the hospital," someone observed.

"Here." Squire appeared beside her, pushing a glass of water into her hand.

"Thank you."

"Had a heart attack once," he said. "Long time ago. How I met my wife, Gloria. Sometimes good things come out of situations like this. Might be the same for that fella tonight. And at least we can offer him hospital care right in town these days." He tapped his chest. "Didn't have that back when I had my bit of difficulty."

"I know you had a lot to do with the hospital being built."

He looked contemplative. "That infernal woman you work for has donated a lot of money to the hospital in the last year."

Penny knew that, too.

"Doesn't mean she knows diddly-squat about what's best for Weaver," he added. "But you can schedule the damn debate."

After the last few minutes, his capitulation seemed much too easy. She gave him a close look. "You'll actually *be* there, right?" she pressed. "I can get the high school auditorium reserved a week before election day."

"If I don't show up, I'll be giving away votes to that termagant you work for." He gave her a twisted smile. "I'll be there," he assured.

Too relieved for words, she pumped his hand with hers. "Thank you, Mr. Clay. Thank you so much!"

He gave a rusty-sounding laugh. "Make it Squire, girl, like everyone else."

"Squire," she repeated with a smile.

He gave her a quick wink before he looped his arm around the teenage pool shark, pulling her over to his side. "Meggie, don't forget your great-grampa, now. I'm expecting a cut o' your winnings."

She looped her arms around his neck, smiling happily. "I won't forget, Grandpa."

Penny smiled around the sudden tightening in her throat. She'd told Vivian she hadn't known her grandparents. She'd long ago convinced herself that it hadn't mattered. But she knew that she never wanted *her* child to believe such a thing. She never wanted her child to feel alone and adrift. She wanted her child to know *family*. Family like the Clays and Templetons—who clearly were always there for one another.

She'd spotted Quinn coming back into the bar and she set aside the water glass, excusing herself.

His dark gaze captured hers when she approached and warmth filled her veins. "How's the man?"

"He'd regained consciousness by the time we got him to the hospital."

She was feeling unaccountably breathless. "So you did go with him?"

"Neither of the deputy sheriffs were EMT certified."

"How'd you get back so fast?"

"Was only a few blocks." His hands closed over her shoulders and slowly ran down her arms. "We have plans."

She let out a faint laugh. "Saving that guy's life is just another day for you."

"Anyone could've done what I did. Basic CPR."

"But anyone *didn't* do what you did."

He lifted his shoulder slightly, looking vaguely self-conscious. It was such an unexpected look on him that she was dangerously charmed. "Least there was more room here than what I'm used to. But then Pave Hawks are a lot better equipped than a barroom floor."

Pave Hawks. He was talking about a helicopter. She knew that from when she'd spent too many sleepless nights reading anything and everything she could find online about the work he did.

"How'd the 'debate' debate go with Squire?"

It took a moment for Penny to drag her thoughts out of the frightening aspects of Quinn's chosen profession. "He, uh, he agreed actually." She gestured at the area where he'd rendered CPR. Tables and chairs and people had already resumed their places, though the voice level had gone up even more. "I think watching all that softened him up or something." She was hyperaware of his hands still moving slowly up and down her arms, though the movements seemed more absent in nature on his part than deliberate. "But whatever the reason, we've got ourselves an official campaign debate. So, happy birthday to me."

Quinn's hands stilled. His eyes stared into hers. "It's your birthday? Why didn't you say so?"

She opened her mouth, but didn't know what to say.

She shrugged. "It's not a big deal. I never celebrate my birthday anyway."

His brows tugged together. "Does Vivian know it's your birthday?"

She spread her hands. "I don't know." Vivian had had her investigated. So she probably did. "It doesn't matter."

"I've got a mother, two sisters and a bunch of female cousins who'd all disagree with you." He closed his hand around one of hers. "Come on."

She realized he was pulling her to the door and quickly grabbed her purse, feeling a sudden panic. Even with the evening's events, she hadn't forgotten that Quinn's presence was only motivated by the pink box that she'd been too much of a ninny to buy for herself. "Where?"

"Dinner."

She lifted her eyebrows, giving their surroundings an obvious look. "This *is* a restaurant."

"And a crowded one where nobody's going to talk about anything but what happened tonight." He kept aiming for the door and a moment later she found herself standing with him on the sidewalk outside the bar and grill.

The silence that descended as soon as the thick door swung closed was deafening in its own way. Now that the sheriff van and its flashing lights were long gone, the street up and down as far as she could see, was entirely quiet.

"There." Quinn smiled down at her. "Isn't that better?"

She wasn't sure that it was. She moistened her lips and edged away slightly in hopes that her nerve endings would stop feeling quite so exhilarated by his nearness. "I don't know. There's a reason Colbys is as crowded as it is. They serve good food there."

"There's good food other places, too," he assured. His

eyes drifted over her, setting off her nerve endings all over again. "You looked pretty in there. Before everything went nuts. I wanted to tell you."

She was suddenly awash in self-consciousness. "I just, uh, blow-dried my hair straight for once."

"It's not the hair," he murmured. He brushed his thumb over her cheek. "Or the paint. It was the smile when you were debating debates with Squire."

She swallowed. "Oh."

"Oh," he parroted with a faint smile. Then his hand grabbed hers again and she realized he was heading toward the same truck he'd had earlier that day.

He'd scored a much closer parking spot to Colbys than she had, too.

Even though she didn't really need help getting up into the high passenger seat, she felt a silly surge of pleasure when he helped her anyway. "Whose truck is this?"

"My cousin's. Same as the motorcycle the other day. Arch collects vehicles like he collects girls." He closed the door and she watched him round the front of the truck.

A moment later he'd gotten behind the wheel, and the spacious cab no longer felt spacious at all. "Do you collect girls, too?"

He gave her a sideways look as he started the truck and drove out onto the quiet street. "Not since I collected a wife."

She pressed her lips together.

"Not going to offer up an argument that you're not my wife?"

She hadn't been going to argue at all. Which was something she wasn't ready to examine. "Would it do any good?"

He shook his head.

She spread her hands as if he'd been the only reason she hadn't argued. "There you go, then." She dropped her hands to her lap and looked out the window. He was driving quickly through downtown, unimpeded by any sort of traffic, and she wondered again where they were heading. "What were you tied up with earlier?"

He glanced at her. He seemed to hesitate for a moment as he looked back to focus on the road. "Had another call from my CO."

His commanding officer. She felt herself tensing. She knew that Quinn's leave had an expiration date that was only getting closer by the minute. "Another call? Sounds ominous. What'd he want?" For him to report back to duty immediately?

"To push the idea of my promotion."

"Promotion!"

His lips twisted. "Sort of. Depends on who you ask. I'm a PJ. I never wanted to be a shirt." His eyes skated briefly over her again. "First Sergeant. It's a special duty assignment. More a position than a rank. If there aren't enough volunteers, then they start looking for volunteers." He grimaced again. "And they started looking."

Andy had talked endlessly about the army. So she knew the army ranks, and assumed the air force ranks weren't significantly different. "That's an important position, isn't it?"

"Yeah. Everyone is the First Sergeant's business. Literally. It's in the creed. First Sergeant is concerned with every detail of every enlisted in the unit. Discipline. Promotion. You name it, they deal with it. And I've had good shirts. And bad ones. The good ones want the position because they really do care about every member of the unit. 24/7. They live for all the paperwork and the hand-holding and the head-knocking that comes with it. The bad ones just care about getting themselves ahead."

"It sounds a lot safer than jumping out of planes and helicopters and God knows what else," she murmured.

"Yeah, well, if the flight surgeon doesn't pass me for flight status at the end of the month, the only thing I might be doing is jumping out of my mind."

Alarm pulsed inside her chest. "You don't need more surgery?"

"Not that kind of surgeon in this case. It's the doctor who can clear me again for flight duty."

That didn't give her any more reason to relax. Flight duty meant he'd be back doing what he loved. "Where do you have to go for that?"

"It's arranged for Warren."

The air force base located near Cheyenne. She chewed the inside of her cheek. "Why do you call them shirts?"

"No idea. We just do." He turned off the road and she frowned, realizing he seemed to be heading in the direction of his grandmother's house.

"Quinn? Why are we heading to Vivian's?"

"Just wait. You'll see."

"Well, I guess I can share the good news with her about Squire agreeing to the debate."

"You can tell her tomorrow. I'm not planning for us to see her."

She raised her eyebrows. "We're going to go to Vivian's. But not see Vivian? Then what *are* we going to do?"

He just smiled.

And she felt it from the top of her suddenly giddy head to the curling in her toes and every point in between.

Happy birthday to her, indeed.

Chapter Thirteen

"This shouldn't taste so good," Penny whispered.

Quinn laughed softly and leaned over the blanket he'd spread on the lush grass to pour more champagne into her glass. The blanket had come from the guesthouse. The champagne from his grandmother's wine cellar. "You don't have to whisper. Sound carries, but I doubt anyone's going to hear us all the way out here."

She looked back at Vivian's house in the distance. It was well illuminated by landscape lights, but where she and Quinn were situated at the farthest point of the manicured grounds, the only light *they* had came from the moon and stars overhead.

"And everything tastes so good," he added, "because a little thievery adds spice to the taste buds."

She couldn't stop a giggle from escaping. "I can't believe Montrose didn't catch us raiding his kitchen." She knew he'd been around, because she'd heard his ponderous footsteps more than once.

"I've raided dicier places than Montrose's kitchen," he assured.

"Yeah, but if he'd caught *you*, what could he say? You're Vivian's grandson. Me, on the other hand? He'd probably find some way to poison me or something." She sipped the champagne. "This is like drinking star-light," she mused.

He laughed softly. "You're drunk on Granny Viv's Perrier Jouet."

She was drunk on *him*, but was fortunately sober enough to keep that point to herself. He'd said one glass wouldn't hurt anything. In case. "I've only had three sips."

She looked into the basket that Quinn had used to gather their purloined meal while she'd played lookout at the kitchen door. They'd had leftover bits of duck con-fit, glazed short ribs, crunchy snow peas and fancy lit-tle twists of asparagus. All cold. All the more delicious because of it.

And because of the thievery.

Smiling to herself, she plucked the last morsel of duck from the plastic container and savored it. "Delicious," she murmured and rolled onto her back to stare up at the stars. "How do Wyoming stars stack up with the rest of the world?

He was stretched out on his back, too. "Up at the top, far as I'm concerned."

She smiled, though it felt more than a little bittersweet. "Only times I've been outside of Wyoming have been because of Vivian's jaunts."

"Las Vegas and Pittsburgh?"

"Mmm-hmm. Well, Colorado, too. We went there in February. She wanted to visit a particular art gallery in Colorado Springs."

"If you could go anywhere in the world, where would you go?"

"Mmm. I dunno," she mused. "I don't waste time on pointless dreams. You, though—I bet I could guess where you'd go." She waved at the stars overhead. "You'd follow the stars across the globe if you could."

"I've already followed the stars across the globe," he murmured. "I'm thinking of following something else these days."

She didn't want to think about where the air force might take him. Her limbs felt like they were melting into the earth beneath them. The night air was still warm with just the vaguest hint of cool sniffing at the edge. And if she wished they could stay right where they were forever, it was her own little secret.

Then she heard the scrape of a match. Smelled the sulfur and turned her lazy head toward Quinn. "Are you smoking?"

She saw the gleam of his smile. He'd sat up. "No." He stuck the end of the wooden matchstick into something and held it out to her. "Happy birthday, Penny Garner. If you won't dream about something, at least make a birthday wish."

He'd pushed the match like a candle into one of Montrose's famous petit fours.

Everything inside her squeezed, then bloomed.

"Be quick," he laughed. "Or it's going to burn out on its own."

She pushed up on her arm and blew out the match.

"Did you make a wish?"

She couldn't do anything but nod. Not without betraying the tears that had flooded her eyes.

"I know it isn't as good as your sixteenth birthday." He plucked the spent match and tossed it into the basket.

His palm was still extended toward her with the frosted confection on it. "But I did what I could."

Her sixteenth birthday. When she'd met Andy.

So much for the tears. They overflowed anyway. She took the tiny square cake and bit off half. It tasted like strawberry. Balanced the other half on the end of two fingers and offered it to him.

"That was for you," he said.

"I know you like them, too," she said huskily.

He smiled slightly and closed his lips over the cake. Over the tips of her fingers.

She sucked in a breath that sounded loud in the night.

He slowly released her fingers. "What did you wish for?"

She curled her fingers against her fist. "If I tell, it won't come true."

It already had, though. She was there. With him.

And she wasn't sure there could be a more perfect birthday.

"Dammit. You're crying."

"I'm not."

"Liar. It's because I brought up your sixteenth."

She shook her head, sitting up and tucking her bare feet under her. Her boots were somewhere at the bottom of the blanket where she'd tossed them. "No, it's not."

"Then why?"

"I'm not used to someone celebrating my birthday."

"Ever?"

She made a sound. "Well, no. I mean—" She broke off. Shook her head.

"The Bennetts celebrated your birthday when you lived with them. Right?"

She thought about the card she'd shoved into her

drawer. "They made a fuss over all of our birthdays. It was just what they did."

"And when you worked for my dad? In the office? No birthday cake in the break room? No card signed by all the staff?"

"And some of the patients," she finished. "We did that with everyone's birthday. Especially your dad's."

"So how can you say nobody celebrates your birthday?"

She opened her mouth. But the right words wouldn't come.

"What did I do wrong to make you cry?"

"Nothing!" She spread her hands. "Don't you see? You did everything right!" So right that she'd almost been able to forget. Her voice felt choked. "Exactly right. But you're going to leave. Just like everyone else I've ever loved. You're going to leave."

He'd gone still.

Only then did she realize what she'd said.

She pushed to her feet. "That didn't come out right," she said brusquely.

She wasn't in love with Quinn.

How could she be?

She swiped her hands down the seat of her pants and looked around for her socks. But despite the moonlight and the stars, it was too dark to see where she'd tossed them.

He stood. "Penny."

She grabbed for one of the dark shadows that was one of her boots. She'd just wear the things without socks if she had to. "We should be getting back."

But he grabbed her arms. "Stop."

Her teeth developed a strange tendency to chatter. She clenched her jaw. "It's late. I'm sure you have stuff to do in the morning same as I do. Your grandmother has a breakfast meeting with the town mayor at seven. It's early, but it was the only time he had available." And of course, there was that damn pink box Quinn had bought for her. Which he still hadn't produced.

Shop-World was open twenty-four hours a day.

She'd just go back there herself and buy one. What was the likelihood of running into someone she knew in the middle of the night?

She realized he was still holding her arms. "Let go, Quinn."

"I'm not sure I can," he murmured cryptically, but he let go of her. "If you're pregnant, Penny, I'm not going to leave."

She winced. "Is that supposed to make me feel better? You'll settle for giving up everything that matters to you just because the stick turns blue?"

"It turns blue?"

She threw out her arms. "I don't know *what* it does. *I* didn't get the test bought, remember?"

He swore under his breath. "This is ridiculous. Put your boots on."

"That's what I was trying to do," she said, feeling entirely frustrated and cranky. Maybe it was hormones.

Pregnancy hormones.

Her eyes burned again as she shoved her bare feet into the boots. Quinn, meanwhile, had bundled everything inside the blanket and thrown it over his shoulder.

Like a bag of garbage.

Sniffing, she stomped off in the direction of Vivian's house. His truck was parked on the side and by the time she reached it, she'd gotten the sniffing under control at least. He opened the truck, but when she went to get inside, he shook his head. He reached in instead, then turned to hand her a small box. "Go on and take the test. Enough waiting." He closed the truck door and headed toward the guesthouse where they'd filched the blanket. "Come on."

Uncertainty threatened to pull her under. She stood there, her fingers rubbing over the sharp edges of the glossy box.

He'd reached the guesthouse. It was typically locked, but he'd gotten it unlocked even without a key and left it that way. Now he stood in the open doorway. "Well?"

She was an adult. She could pee on a damn stick. She stiffened her spine and marched toward him.

He flipped on a lamp inside the guesthouse and without looking at him, she closed herself in the bathroom where at least she didn't have to have him witness the way her fingers shook as she peeled open the box and read the directions. There was no turning blue. Just one line or two.

He knocked on the door, startling her, and she dropped the box.

"You need help in there?" he said through the door.

"No." She picked up the box. Pulled out one of the tests.

"It's only supposed to take a minute for the results to show."

"Do *you* want to pee on it?" She remembered the way he'd barged in on her in Vegas and hastily pushed the lock button on the doorknob.

"That dinky lock wouldn't stop me for ten seconds."

"Hush up!" Her reflection in the mirror showed her face to be just as flushed as she'd feared. Now that it was time to do the deed, she wasn't sure that she was even going to be able to pee. "And don't stand there at the door listening, either." She flipped on the water faucet for good measure. It was juvenile, maybe, but she couldn't stand thinking that he'd hear anything she did in there.

She tore open the wrapper and closed her eyes, taking a deep breath. Then she sat and tinkled on the stick.

She put the cap on the stick and set it on the edge of the sink. Flushed the toilet and washed her hands. Turned off the water and unlocked the door.

She stared at the line creeping across the result window.

The door opened behind her. "Well?"

She realized she was holding her breath.

He joined her in front of the sink. His arm brushed against hers as they watched. And waited.

He looked at the sturdy black watch with the complicated dial strapped on his wrist.

They waited some more.

She finally exhaled. It was either that, or pass out. "Only one line."

He picked up the directions. Glanced through them and looked at the test again. "I thought for sure it would be positive."

She swallowed the knot in her throat and briskly wrapped the negative test in tissue paper and shoved it in the trash beneath the sink. "Well, now you can stop worrying."

"How many days late are you?"

"Four."

"We should've just done a blood test. It would be more accurate. Maybe it's too early."

"It's negative," she said flatly. "I'm not pregnant." She ought to be relieved.

Why wasn't she relieved?

Happy birthday to me.

Her vision blurred and she stuffed the directions back

into the box with the second, unused test that was obviously unnecessary, and dumped it, too, in the trash. "If you wouldn't mind dropping me off at Colbys, my car is still parked there."

"Penny. We need to talk about this."

"What's there to talk about?" She brushed past him as she went back into the living area of the guesthouse. He'd left the blanket-wrapped bundle containing evidence of their thievery on one of the upholstered chairs situated in front of a fireplace. "I'm not pregnant. There's no reason for you to feel responsible for me. So I'll get that paperwork filled out for you for the lawyer." There was a buzzing in her head and a pain in her chest.

Maybe at thirty, she was going to have a heart attack.

Quinn could give her CPR. Be the hero that he always would be.

"I'm not worried about that damn paperwork." His voice was tight.

"No." She waved an arm. "You're worried about getting okayed for flight duty so you can go back to Afghanistan or Pakistan or whatever other Danger-Stan you can go back to. And the only reason you're preoccupied with *me* is because it's better than thinking about the alternative facing you. Being a *shirt*. Or getting out altogether."

"The only reason I'm preoccupied with *you*, is because I can't get you out from under my skin! You're my *wife*."

She trembled. "Not intentionally."

"Fine. Is this *intentional* enough for you?" His mouth slammed down onto hers.

She went rigid.

He lifted his head, muttering a curse, and ran his fingers through her hair. "You're killing me, Penny." Then his mouth found hers again. Slowly. Gently. His fingers stroked down her cheeks. "Kiss me back, sweetheart. Just once."

He tasted like champagne and the faint sweetness of strawberry.

And his lips were so soft. So tempting.

"Don't think," he murmured. His mouth moved. He kissed her eyes closed. First one. Then the other. "Just feel." His lips returned to hers, barely grazing them. "That's all you have to do, sweetheart. Just feel."

Her fingers flexed against his waist.

He didn't realize that *feel* was all she could do anyway.

She could feel his breath mixing with hers. Could feel her knees weakening. Her resistance melting away as if it had never existed at all.

"I'm not going anywhere," he whispered.

Not yet.

The words circled inside her head but didn't gain enough momentum to find voice.

And then, without intention, her hands were moving up his chest. Circling his neck. Fingers sliding through his hair and her mouth opened under his.

She felt his arms surround her, cradling her close. Then closer still. And there was so much feeling that she was afraid it was going to explode out of her chest.

But then he swore. Peeled her away from him.

She stared wordlessly at him.

"I don't have anything with me." His voice sounded deep. "And taking another spin at that particular roulette would be irresponsible."

"I don't care," she whispered.

His eyes darkened even more. "Penny."

Then she remembered. "My purse."

His eyebrows lifted.

"Wait." Before she lost her nerve, she ran out to the

truck. Grabbed her purse that was still sitting on the floor where she'd left it and rummaged inside for the forgotten box of condoms. She ran back into the guesthouse, holding it up. Her burst of triumph popped, though, under the surprised look he gave her.

"I, uh, I bought them by mistake," she muttered.

"Divine mistake," he said, smiling slowly as he reached for her again, sweeping her right off her feet.

"Quinn! I'm too tall for this."

He laughed softly. "That's what you say? You're supposed to swoon with delight or something." Her boots knocked against the wall as he carried her down the short hallway and into the bedroom where the only light came from the gleam of the moon through the uncovered window.

She *was* swooning.

He set her on the side of the bed. Took the box from her hands and pulled out one of the foil-wrapped packets. Then he crouched before her and slowly pulled off her boots. Unfastened her jeans and slid them down her legs. Pulled her T-shirt over her head. And when she wore nothing but her bra and panties, he stood in front of her, a tall, broad shadow of a man and pulled off his own clothes. He ripped open the foil.

Shadowy or not, the sight still made her breath stop in her chest. But then he came down beside her on the bed and kissed her again and she forgot about breathing and she forgot about everything outside that moment. Outside that room.

He had magic hands. Magic lips. Her bra and panties went astray while he wound the need inside her tighter and tighter. Even greedier for more, she pulled him over her, arching against him. This time...this time...

she would remember every breath. Every sigh. Every movement.

He rocked his hips into hers, slowly filling her. Stretching her. Her mind reeled and she whispered his name, only to jerk with the quick, sharp pain that was gone almost as soon as it came.

But above her, Quinn froze.

His fingers threaded through hers. "I hurt you."

"No." She could feel the pulsing heat of him inside her and she reached up to find his mouth with hers. Everything inside her yearned. "It was just a second. It's gone, Quinn. I promise. Don't stop."

"I couldn't stop if I wanted." His breath was a hiss between his teeth. "You were still a virgin."

She pressed her mouth against his hot throat. Everything inside her wanted more. "I already admitted that. Until Las Vegas—"

"Until now." He pressed his forehead against hers. "Until now, Penny. We never made love in Las Vegas at all. Not completely. Not like now. Nothing happened that you didn't want."

She pushed her hands against his chest, staring into his eyes even though it was too dark to see properly. "I told you before you wouldn't have done anything like that." She didn't believe anything could change the intrinsic decency that ran inside him as surely as the blood in his veins. "Stop thinking about it." Then she pressed her mouth to his and wound her legs higher around his hips.

He let out a low laugh. "I can't think about anything when you do that."

Her heart was thundering. "Good," she managed breathlessly. "At least now we have a wedding night I can remember."

He went still. She could feel his heart beating as

clearly as she could feel her own. Could feel the pulse of him so deep inside her, she knew she would never feel the same again.

"Then I'd better make it really memorable." His hands tightened around her, and he moved intently.

Just feel, he'd said. That was all she could do, then. Until feeling turned to need that spun her into a kaleidoscope of pleasure.

The angle of moonlight slowly shifted across the bed as they lay there afterward.

"I wish there'd have been two lines," he said into the dark.

Her eyes flooded. She couldn't take it. Not when her body was still humming, feeling forever changed.

Two lines and he would have stayed with her no matter what.

"So do I." Three words had never felt so momentous.

And if she started crying, she was afraid she might not ever stop. She cleared her throat and abruptly scooted off the bed. "But there weren't two lines." Her foot landed on her clothes and she blindly scooped everything up in her arms.

She rushed out of the room and into the bathroom. She dropped the bundle of clothes on the floor and pawed through them for her bra and panties. She found the panties. Not the bra. But she wasn't going back into that bedroom no matter what. And it wasn't exactly the first time she'd had to leave Quinn's bed without her underwear.

She felt a hysterical laugh bubbling in her chest as she grabbed the blue jeans. Only they weren't her jeans. They were his. How she'd managed not to notice was a testament to her lack of functioning brain cells. She actually shook them out, considering them for size.

But they were a good half foot too long. Several inches

too wide. She jerkily rolled them into a ball and tossed them onto the sink. The pings as change fell out of his pocket sounded loud and muttering under her breath, she moved the jeans to retrieve them. The last thing she needed was to stop up a drain in Vivian's guesthouse.

But as she reached for the small collection of quarters and dimes and pennies lying in the white porcelain sink, she saw a glint of gold. A sparkle of diamond.

Her fingers trembled as she slid the ring away from the coins.

Quinn was carrying her wedding band around in his pocket.

She picked it up. Felt vaguely insane as she slid it onto her ring finger.

"Penny." He knocked on the door and she jumped like she'd been bit when the door opened a millisecond later. "You've got my jeans."

She flushed, literally caught red-handed and red-faced.

He was boldly, beautifully naked and her plain white bra was dangling from his finger.

She snatched it away. "*Knock* next time."

His gaze was focused on the ring she'd found. The ring that shouldn't be on her finger at all.

"If I knocked, think of all the interesting things I'd miss."

Her hands shook as she pulled on her clothes, because it was plainly obvious that he wasn't going to look away just because she was blushing like the thirty-year-old virgin she no longer was. And maybe he could stand there all naked like that, but *she* couldn't.

She pulled off the ring and held it out to him.

"I like it better on your finger."

She swallowed hard. "We might have had a wedding, but I'm not your wife, Quinn. It was all just one big mistake. You know that. I know that. We need to stop pretending. Stop playing."

"I was never playing."

Her knees were still mush. She pressed her lips together and prayed that he'd take the ring before she lost it altogether. "What you want and what I want are too different."

He slowly took the ring. It fit over the very tip of his thumb but went no farther. He held it up between them. "I want things in my life that matter. You matter."

Her eyes stung. "We don't love each other. We...we hardly know each other."

"Keep telling yourself that, sweetheart. Maybe it will start to ring true eventually. I've known you half your life." He ran his thumb and the ring over her cheek. "And if there's one thing I want for you, it's that you'd remember that dreams are never pointless."

She clenched her teeth together.

Then he reached past her for his jeans. "I'll take you back to your car."

And back to reality.

Chapter Fourteen

"Mail for you." Quinn's cousin, Archer, tossed an envelope down in front of him as he came in the front door of his house. He'd been out running and sweat was running down his face. "I'm hitting the shower. Then you want to go grab a beer?"

It was rare for Arch to be around at all between his various travels to and from Denver and Cheyenne and elsewhere. But it was the middle of the afternoon. It was hot. And a beer sounded good.

"Sure." Quinn didn't have anything else in particular to do. And a beer was better than moping.

He waited until his cousin had left the room again before reaching for the manila envelope sitting on the coffee table where Arch had tossed it. He recognized the return address as the one belonging to the lawyer handling his and Penny's divorce.

He peeled open the envelope and slid out the documents.

She'd signed them already.

They were dated two weeks ago.

She must have submitted them the day after her birthday.

The day after they'd made love.

He sighed.

He hadn't seen her since that night. Hadn't talked to her. Not because he didn't want to. But because he didn't know what else there was to say.

He read through the papers.

In the state of Wyoming, when the parties were in agreement and there were no children involved, it was a depressingly easy and quick matter to undo one's marriage vows.

Even ones of the forgotten Vegas variety.

He went and found a pen in Arch's office and returned to the couch where he'd been spending way too much time lately. He spread the sheets of paper across the coffee table. Clicked the pen a few times.

He was still staring at the red sticky flag that pointed to the line where he was supposed to sign when Archer came back in the room.

He flopped down into the chair next to the couch and rubbed his towel over his blond head. "That the paperwork for your next assignment?"

"No." His physical with the flight surgeon had come and gone.

Quinn didn't need to bow to pressure about the First Sergeant deal. Because the flight surgeon had cleared him for flight duty.

The PJ was still a PJ. And his CO needed him in that position more than he needed a shirt. All Quinn needed now were orders for his next assignment, which could arrive in two days or twenty.

He rolled the pen between his fingers. "They're my divorce papers."

Arch pulled the towel away from his head. He gave Quinn a long look. "Been hiding a wife all these years?"

Quinn's lips twisted. He tossed down the pen and leaned back against the couch, stretching his arms behind his head. The twinge in his side was still there. But it was no longer bad enough to end his career. "Only the last month."

Archer wadded up the towel and pitched it across the room onto the breakfast counter. He combed his fingers through his damp hair and stood. "Come on." He grabbed the truck keys from the table by the door. "I have the feeling this is going to take more than a beer."

It took considerably more.

Even though Quinn had matched his cousin whiskey shot for whiskey shot as he'd relayed the framework of his and Penny's marital mess, he still didn't feel any mercifully numbing effects.

They were the only ones sitting at the bar at a place called Magic Jax. Which meant Jax wasn't having a lot of magic on Tuesdays the way that Colbys did over in Weaver.

Quinn tipped the bottle over his shot glass one more time. The bartender had just left the entire bottle to them and was sitting on a bar stool in the corner watching a dinky television and sipping soda through a straw.

"She's still in love with a kid who has a halo on his head."

Arch reached over the bar for the container of peanuts and pretzels and refilled the bowl in front of them for about the third time since they'd gotten there. "From everything you've said about her life, can you blame her? I remember all those foster kids living across from you.

It was like watching a clown car. The front door would open and people just kept pouring out."

It was an apt description. But then his cousin was a lawyer. He was supposed to be good with words.

"If you are right, then she's in love with a memory," Arch added. "And a memory doesn't keep your toes toasty at night or add little germ pods who call you mommy or daddy."

Quinn winced. He'd told Archer about the wedding. Not about the entire pregnancy deal. "I can remember the wedding like it was yesterday."

"Sure that's not from watching that DVD?"

He shouldn't have admitted that he'd gotten another copy of the wedding DVD from Happily Ever Chapel.

"I'm a little wounded, though," Arch said around a mouthful of pretzels. "You go to a *stranger* to handle the divorce?"

"I told you. She didn't want anyone to know."

Arch nodded. "Women be crazy that way." He squinted as he lifted his shot glass. "To your A-OK from the good air force doctor," he said more or less clearly.

Quinn tapped his shot glass against his. "Right." He felt the sideways look his cousin gave him. "What?"

"Your life's gonna be back to normal, Sarge. That's what you want, right?"

"Yup." He nodded. Twisted the shot glass between his fingers. "Normal." He was pretty sure nothing was going to feel normal for a very, very long time.

"Granny Viv's debate is tonight."

Quinn nodded again. The debate that would never have come about if not for Penny's efforts. "Yup."

Arch slapped his shoulder. "We should go."

Magic Jax was only a couple blocks from Archer's

house. "Better walk," Quinn said. Neither one of them was sober enough to drive even a short distance.

"Helluva long walk to Weaver, boy-o."

"Weaver. Who said anything about Weaver?"

"I did. And you know you want to go, even though you're too much of a girl to admit it. Man up a little, wouldja? You're a disgrace to the entire macho breed." Archer pulled out his wallet and extracted several bills. He tossed them on the bar. "Come on."

"You don't handle enough driving-while-intoxicated, you want to add ourselves to your caseload?"

Archer made a face. "Have I taught you nothing?" He'd already pulled out his cell phone. "Maddie," he said a moment later. He grinned at Quinn. "How'd you like to do your big brother a little favor?"

Quinn shook his head. "I can't believe you called your sister for a ride," he said once Archer hung up.

"She's on her way," he said, looking satisfied. He paused for a moment. "You just need to propose to Penny."

Quinn jerked. "What?"

"Propose," Arch said blithely. As though he was an authority on the subject. "Down on one knee. Give her a ring. The whole bit."

Arch wasn't an authority on proposals. Propositions? That was a different story. "I gave her a ring. She gave it back." It was still in Quinn's pocket. A constant reminder of what they might have had.

"Yeah, well, she can't remember you offering it to her in the first place, can she? Y'all just woke up married. *Fait accompli.*"

"She's not in love with me. She said so." She'd also implied that she did.

Arch was waving his hand, dismissing that. "Women

say that all the time. In my experience, if they take the trouble to say it, they rarely mean it."

Quinn snorted. "I see the years haven't made you any more modest."

"Waste of time." Arch pointed. "There's Maddie's car."

The conservative sedan pulled up at the curb a moment later and they piled in. Archer in the front. Quinn in the back. "You boys smell like a distillery," Maddie told them. "Fortunately, I came prepared." She handed them both tall thermoses of hot coffee.

"S'why you're my favorite little sister, Maddie." Archer grinned over his shoulder at Quinn.

"And when Ali's doing you a favor, she's your favorite," Maddie said drily. "Same with Greer. You're not fooling anyone, brother dear. But as it happens, I don't mind driving either one of you to Weaver, because I want to see Vivian's debate, too." She looked at Quinn through the rearview mirror. "Congrats on the flight status, by the way."

"News travels fast in this town." He'd only gotten the clearance a few days earlier.

"You wanna talk about news." Arch leaned toward Maddie as he fastened his seat belt while she pulled away from the curb. "Quinn's got juicier news 'n that."

Quinn leaned his head against the back of the seat and closed his eyes. "Shut up, Archer."

He heard his cousin laughing silently. But at least he didn't spill the beans to his sister. So maybe his lawyer cousin wasn't too far gone on the pain-in-the-ass scale.

Propose to Penny.

What good would it do? He'd already told her how he'd felt. He'd gotten an envelope full of divorce papers as a result.

Maddie seemed to know all the details about the debate already, and drove straight to the high school in less than an hour.

"Wow," Maddie murmured as she drove around looking for a vacant spot. "Never underestimate a local election's importance." She ended up parking down the street from the school.

She had no way of knowing just how close to Penny's house that was.

He could see the porch light burning in the front of the white and yellow bungalow. She wouldn't be there, of course. She was Vivian's right-hand woman. She would naturally be at the debate.

They got out of the car. Maddie and Archer headed one way toward the school.

He set off the other way toward Penny's house. He heard Maddie call his name. Archer telling her to let him go.

He broke into a jog after a few yards. Then a run.

He could have run for miles without breaking a sweat. But he felt breathless when he reached her front porch and pulled open the screen door. There was no way she'd be there. He knocked anyway.

The door suddenly opened and she stood there. The woman who was his wife in none of the ways that mattered.

She was wearing a thin pink robe that left way too little to his imagination and holding something black and sequined in her hands.

"Sequins look pretty fancy for a town council debate."

The shock in her translucent blue eyes disappeared like a snap.

She tossed the sequined garment aside but didn't move an inch out of the doorway as she folded her arms over her chest. It did nothing but accentuate the lush curves beneath her robe, which he was certain had *not* been her intention. "What are you doing here? If this is about the divorce papers, you could've just sent them back to the lawyer."

"I don't want a divorce. I want to marry my wife."

Her lips parted. Color drained out of her face. Then it climbed just as quickly back up her long, lovely throat. "You had your appointment with the flight surgeon, I guess."

"That doesn't have anything to do with me being here."

"Hey there, Penny!"

He jerked around to see a round, red-haired woman striding down the street with a skinny bald guy by her side, watching them unashamedly. "Going to see you at the debate, I'm sure?"

Penny nodded. "Hi, Dori. Yes, I'll be there."

The woman looked like she would have stopped and waited for Penny right then and there, if not for the skinny guy pulling her arm to keep on moving.

Quinn turned his back on them, focusing on Penny.

She moistened her lips, looking away. She kept one hand wrapped around herself, but grabbed the door with the other. Preparing to close it in his face, maybe.

He put his foot in the doorway. Just in case.

But it also brought him closer to her.

He heard the breath she inhaled before she took a step back.

"Quinn, I can't do this. I'm going to be late for the debate."

"You were already late for the debate before I got here. Another few minutes aren't going to matter."

She looked pained.

"Are you going to let me in, or are we going to do this on your front porch?"

"Do what?"

He pulled the wedding ring out of his pocket. She'd chosen it at Happily Ever Chapel. Something inside her had to remember that. Even subconsciously. He dropped down to one knee.

She gaped. "What are you *doing*?" She dragged at his shoulders. "Get up before someone else sees you."

So much for going on one knee. It hadn't worked to get him a kiss that time she'd been mowing her lawn, and it wasn't getting him any further with a proposal now. "This knee business is for the birds," he muttered, straightening. He stepped forward, nudging her far enough backward that he could slam the door on the outside world.

She tried to pull away from him, but he held fast. "I am in love with you," he said bluntly. "That's the only reason I'm here. Not because of Las Vegas. Though if what happened there hadn't happened there, it might have taken us a little longer to get to this point."

He could feel the fine tremble that worked through her. "We're not at *any* point, Quinn! The divorce papers just need your signature."

"And I'll sign the damn things if it means I can marry you the way I want to!"

Her expression pinched. "S-stop saying that!"

"Why? You don't like hearing the truth?"

She blinked. Swiped at her cheek and tried to pull away from him yet again. "You wanted me to have a dream, Quinn? Well, the only dream I have is not being second choice. Not *your* second choice."

"Who the hell am I supposed to choose above you?" His voice was rising and he couldn't seem to do a damn thing to stop it. "You're the only woman I've ever *met* who makes me want something that I've never wanted before. And it took a grenade nearly blowing me up to come back to find you."

"Not who. What! You were a PJ! I know what that meant to you. And now because of that grenade you can't be one, and you've had a glimpse of fatherhood and decided hey, that might not be such a bad alternative, so you—"

He covered her mouth with his hand.

Her eyes flashed at him. She said something against his palm that she probably hadn't said since she'd been fifteen and furious as hell with him.

"I *am* a pararescueman," he said. "I got signed off for duty last week. But I know how you feel about hitching your wagon to a military man. Which is why I'm putting in for reassignment." The decision was so freaking easy now that he'd made it, he couldn't figure why it had taken him this long. "I'll ride a desk. I'll teach. I'll talk to my shirt and figure out anything that'll keep me Stateside and safe as houses. I can get retirement at twenty years. That's only eighteen months away, sweetheart. We can get married then if you want. But if you can't wait that long, or you won't wait even two minutes, I'll get out now. I'm a paramedic. I'll find a job. I'll support you. I'll support our kids. I'll do anything it takes. But if you say one more time that you're anything but my *first* choice—my *first* priority—I'm gonna put you over my knee the way somebody should have done when you were fifteen!"

She'd gone still. Her eyes were liquid blue saucers above his hand.

He hauled in a deep breath. "I haven't had anything mess with my head as bad as you since I was going through Indoc, when I first enlisted a long damn time ago." He pulled his hand away from her mouth. "And I've never had anyone mess with my heart the way you do. Just give me a chance to make you happy, Penny. That's all I'm asking for here."

Her eyes overflowed. "You were cleared for flight duty."

"You're missing the point, sweetheart."

She shook her head. Swiped her cheeks. "I can't ask you to make that choice."

He lifted her chin. Looked into her eyes. "There is no choice, Penny. Don't you get it yet? There's only you. I choose you. I choose *us*."

"But the paperwork—"

"Do we really have to divorce each other just so we can get married the right way?"

There was a tremulous smile finally growing on her lips. Enough of one that he drew his first easy breath in the last two weeks. "I'm used to convoluted reasoning when it comes to the military, so I suppose I—"

She covered his mouth with her palm. "I choose you, too, Quinn."

Relief was a wave rolling over him. "You'll marry me."

She held out her left hand. It was shaking. "I already did. The night you put that beautiful band on my finger."

His throat felt tight. He slid the ring into place. Lifted her hand and kissed it. "Tell me you love me." He needed to hear the words.

"I was crazy about you when I was fifteen. I'm crazy about you still." She slid her hand behind his neck, pressing herself against him as she stretched up to his mouth. "I love you, Quinn Templeton. Now." She punctuated it with a brush of her lips against his. "Always." Another kiss. "I just have one request."

"Anything." Whatever she wanted, he'd find a way to

make it work. He was a man used to using any means at his disposal to meet his objective. And his objective had never been more important.

She linked her other hand with his and drew it around her waist, beneath the robe. Her eyes turned to sapphire. "I want another wedding night," she whispered.

He spread his fingers against her smooth, beautiful skin. "Now?"

She nodded. "Now."

"What about Vivian's debate?"

She smiled softly and pulled his head toward hers. "I think more than anyone else, Vivian will understand."

And then she kissed him.

Epilogue

"I always knew you'd make a beautiful bride."

Penny looked over to see Susie Bennett's familiar face. She'd told Quinn that morning that she wasn't going to do any more crying. Because she was too happy.

But her eyes stung anyway.

"Can I come in?"

Penny nodded wordlessly and Susie entered the bedroom Penny was using to get ready for her wedding redo with Quinn. Susie pushed the door closed behind her. Then she just stood there, hands clasped in front of her. "Well," she finally said thickly. "I met Mrs. Templeton. She's quite something."

Penny finally let out a choked laugh. She nodded. "Vivian *is* something, all right." She'd turned her household almost upside down in the past month so that her grandson and Penny could have the small wedding that they wanted. Just because something was small, Vivian had claimed, was no reason it shouldn't be absolutely perfect. She'd even manipulated Montrose into preparing a feast for their reception.

And she'd sent a charter plane to Florida to make sure George and Susie Bennett would be there.

"You look happy," Susie said.

"I am." Penny suddenly reached out and took the other woman's hands. "I'm sorry," she said huskily. "So sorry."

Susie shook her head and wrapped her in a swift hug. "Oh, honey." She rocked her the same way she'd rocked her when she'd been just a girl. "You have nothing to be sorry for."

"I shouldn't have shut you out the way I did. I kept all your cards. Everything." She'd finally opened each one. With Quinn sitting beside her, she'd read every word in every card and letter from the past ten years. Because of him, she'd finally found peace. Because of him, she'd found everything she'd ever wanted. "You were so good to me. To Andy. To everyone and I—"

"Shh." Susie hushed her. "No more sorries. I'm just so glad you wanted us here. This is a day to celebrate." She kissed her forehead and pulled back, holding Penny's hands wide. "You can't walk down the aisle with red eyes."

"No, she certainly can't." Vivian had stuck her head around the door. "Mind if we come in?"

Penny smiled when she saw the little boy dressed in a miniature suit and bow tie accompanying Vivian and Delia. Her young sister-in-law had warned her that she'd be bringing Matty to the wedding. She was watching him for the week while Margaret and her husband were gone for a second honeymoon. They'd been spending a lot of time at Vivian's, since Delia had quit her job at Braden Drugs.

Penny crouched down to Matty's level. "Hi, Matty. Can I have a kiss?"

He gave her his toothy grin and a wet kiss on the lips and her heart turned over. If she and Quinn were lucky, maybe they'd have a Matty of their own in the making very soon.

"All right, Matty. Come on." Delia held out her hand for the tot. "I'll get him settled with my mom and be back up in a sec." She was acting as Penny's maid of honor while Quinn's dad was standing up for him as best man.

"Sounds good." She watched them go. If Penny's plan worked, Delia would find herself in another job, this time working for Vivian as Penny's replacement. She'd already put some of the plan to work.

So far, Vivian seemed to find her flighty granddaughter a good project to focus on after narrowly losing the town council seat to Squire Clay.

"I came in to tell you that Mr. Morales has arrived," Vivian told her. "He's quite charming." She made as much of a face as she ever would. "But he really has the most dreadfully dyed hair. He and Quinn are all ready when you are."

Penny smiled at her boss. At her grandmother by marriage. "Thank you for indulging us."

"Ah." Vivian looked pleased as she waved away the comment. "It's *your* wedding." She linked her arm through Susie's. Two women who couldn't seem more different, who meant so much to Penny. "Let's get going, shall we? Montrose has been very even keeled so far today and it's probably to our benefit to keep him that way by having the ceremony reasonably on time. I do want to know more about the charity your husband was telling me about," she said as they left. "I understand you're looking for some funding. My dear Arthur had a fondness for sea turtles." Vivian looked over her shoulder at Penny and gave her a quick wink as she closed the door.

Penny exhaled. Swiped a fresh rush of tears away from her face and quickly redid her mascara.

Then she stepped back from the full-length mirror and checked her reflection.

The dress Maggie Clay had made for her this time was simple. Just a strapless lace bodice and a long sweep of blush-colored chiffon with a ribbon at her waist. Perfectly suited for their small outdoor wedding.

The bedroom door opened again and she turned, expecting to see Delia again.

But it was her groom who slipped inside the bedroom and closed the door.

Quinn wore his service blues and even though she'd been prepared, it was still an awesome sight. "Vivian was right," she murmured. "The uniform is pretty impressive." She held out the skirt of her dress. "But you're not supposed to see the bride in her wedding gown before the wedding."

He smiled slowly. "Yeah, but this is take two, Mrs. Templeton."

"Oh, that's right." She stroked her hand down the front of his uniform. "Does that mean no more wedding nights?"

"You want a wedding night every night, I'm your man." He caught her hand before she could get to exploring too much. He kissed her fingertips. "You're still sure?"

"About marrying my husband? Very."

"About moving to Lackland for a few months."

She rubbed her fingers over his chin. It was rare for him to be so clean-shaven. "You'll be a very good PJ instructor." She reached up to kiss his chin. "They're going to want to keep you for more than a few months."

"That's all they're going to get. We're coming back to Wyoming soon as everything is set for me to work for the hospital."

Not only the hospital. He'd be doing search and rescue for the state, as well. She stretched a little farther to find his lips. They'd gone over the plan again and again as he'd worked out the details of finishing his service so he wouldn't lose his retirement. "Totally unnecessary 911 calls will increase just because all the women around here'll want to see their favorite paramedic in action." She tugged on his tie. "Kiss me."

"If I kiss you like you're tempting me to, we'll be late for our own wedding."

She glanced over her shoulder toward the window that overlooked the grass where the few dozen chairs were already filled by their guests. The breeze was light. The sky blue. "That probably would be bad," she murmured.

"Worse than you missing Vivian's debate," he agreed.

"On the other hand," she murmured, "it's the perfect time of the month to try and make two lines show up on the stick next time…"

He laughed softly and locked the door.

* * * * *

Don't miss these other stories in New York Times
and USA TODAY *bestselling author Allison Leigh's
long-running* RETURN TO THE DOUBLE C *series:*

THE RANCHER'S DANCE
COURTNEY'S BABY PLAN
A WEAVER PROPOSAL
A WEAVER VOW
A WEAVER BEGINNING
A WEAVER CHRISTMAS GIFT
ONE NIGHT IN WEAVER
THE BFF BRIDE
A CHILD UNDER HIS TREE

Available from Mills & Boon Cherish.

MILLS & BOON®

Cherish™

EXPERIENCE THE ULTIMATE RUSH OF FALLING IN LOVE

A sneak peek at next month's titles...

In stores from 10th August 2017:

- **Sarah and the Secret Sheikh** – Michelle Douglas *and* **Romancing the Wallflower** – Michelle Major
- **A Proposal from the Crown Prince** – Jessica Gilmore *and* **A Wedding to Remember** – Joanna Sims

In stores from 24th August 2017:

- **Her New York Billionaire** – Andrea Bolter *and* **The Waitress's Secret** – Kathy Douglass
- **Conveniently Engaged to the Boss** – Ellie Darkins *and* **The Maverick's Bride-to-Order** – Stella Bagwell

---

Just can't wait?
Buy our books online before they hit the shops!
www.millsandboon.co.uk

Also available as eBooks.

MILLS & BOON®

EXCLUSIVE EXTRACT

Artist Holly Motta arrives in New York to find billionaire Ethan Benton in the apartment where *she's* meant to be staying! And the next surprise? Ethan needs a fake fiancée and he wants *her* for the role…

Read on for a sneak preview of
HER NEW YORK BILLIONAIRE
by debut author Andrea Bolter

"In exchange for you posing as my fiancée, as I have outlined, you will be financially compensated and you will become legal owner of this apartment and any items such as clothes and jewels that have been purchased for this position. Your brother's career will not be impacted negatively should our work together come to an end. *And…*" He paused for emphasis.

Holly leaned forward in her chair, her back still board-straight.

"I have a five-building development under construction in Chelsea. There will be furnished apartments, office lofts and common space lobbies – all in need of artwork. I will commission you for the project."

Holly's lungs emptied. A commission for a big corporate project. That was exactly what she'd hoped she'd find in New York. A chance to have her work seen by thousands of people. The kind of exposure that could lead from one job to the next and to a sustained and successful career.

This was all too much. Fantastic, frightening, impossible… Obviously getting involved in any way with Ethan Benton was a terrible idea. She'd be beholden to him. Serving another person's agenda again. Just what she'd come to New York to get away from.

But this could be a once-in-a-lifetime opportunity. An apartment. A job. It sounded as if he was open to most any demand she could come up with. She really did owe it to herself to contemplate this opportunity.

Her brain was no longer operating normally. The clock on Ethan's desk reminded her that it was after midnight. She'd left Fort Pierce early that morning.

"That really is an incredible offer..." She exhaled. "But I'm too tired to think straight. I'm going to need to sleep on it."

"As you wish."

Holly moved to collect the luggage she'd arrived with. Ethan beat her to it and hoisted the duffle bag over his shoulder. He wrenched the handle of the suitcase. Its wheels tottered as fast as her mind whirled as she followed him to the bedroom.

"Goodnight, then." He placed the bags just inside the doorway and couldn't get out of the room fast enough.

Before closing the door she poked her head out and called, "Ethan Benton, you don't play fair."

Over his shoulder, he turned his face back toward her. "I told you. I always get what I want."

Don't miss
HER NEW YORK BILLIONAIRE
by exciting new author
Andrea Bolter

Available September 2017
www.millsandboon.co.uk

MILLS & BOON®

Why shop at millsandboon.co.uk?

Each year, thousands of romance readers
find their perfect read at millsandboon.co.uk.
That's because we're passionate about
bringing you the very best romantic fiction.
Here are some of the advantages of
shopping at www.millsandboon.co.uk:

* **Get new books first**—you'll be able to buy
  your favourite books one month before they
  hit the shops

* **Get exclusive discounts**—you'll also be
  able to buy our specially created monthly
  collections, with up to 50% off the RRP

* **Find your favourite authors**—latest news,
  interviews and new releases for all your
  favourite authors and series on our website,
  plus ideas for what to try next

* **Join in**—once you've bought your favourite
  books, don't forget to register with us to rate,
  review and join in the discussions

Visit **www.millsandboon.co.uk**
for all this and more today!